Sunsets in Oia

Sheila Busteed

Produced by·

FriesenPress

Suite 300 – 852 Fort Street
Victoria, BC, Canada V8W 1H8

www.friesenpress.com

Distributed to the trade by The Ingram Book Company

To my sister, Erin…
…with more love and admiration
than is possible to describe.

Santorini and the village of Oia:

an introduction

When travellers envision Greece, one of the first images that inevitably pop into their minds is that of the white-washed buildings and blue-domed churches in the picturesque village of Oia (pro-nounced *EE-ah*). Located at the northern tip of the crescent-shaped island of Santorini, one of the southernmost Greek islands in the Aegean Sea, Oia is known around the world for its spectacular sunset and its fascinating history.

Oia was a major hub for Hellenic sea merchants. Ships' captains built their lavish Venetian homes at the top of the cliffs and spent their downtime there between trade trips to Alexandria, Russia and various European ports.

Known to the Greeks as Thira, the island of Santorini offers a wonderful backdrop for the village of Oia. Rising sharply out of the sea, the island curls around an ancient and still-active volcano that dwells below the deep waters of a caldera. While much of Greece struggles with the current financial crisis, Santorini continues to thrive thanks to a busy tourism industry, the production of exceptional wine and the harvesting of delicious local foods. Artists also flock to the island for the abundant inspiration.

The island is also steeped in rich folklore. Many locals and historians suggest that Thira is intimately linked to the lost island of Atlantis. At the height of the Minoan civilization, trade routes had been established between many Aegean islands, including Santorini. A relic of that age – the island's ancient ruins at Akrotiri – shows that people were living in multi-level structures that featured indoor plumbing and other supposedly modern luxuries more than 3600 years ago. Remnants of that time were preserved when the volcano erupted violently and buried the town. The stark similarities between ancient Akrotiri and the rumoured lifestyle on Atlantis suggest that the two communities were at least trading partners. Some people have gone so far as to speculate that Santorini could be what's left of Atlantis itself.

Chapter One

The scruffy, old driver pulled the beat-up, rusty taxi over to one side of the village's bus depot, which was little more than an oversized cul-de-sac. As he turned to face Selene, she caught a whiff of him – stale body odour, cheap cologne, olive oil and tobacco. It triggered memories of her grandfather. He looked her up and down briefly and then said, with a thick Greek islander accent, "Welcome to Oia." *He sounds like he doesn't practice his English much.* She pulled a few bills from her purse and, as she handed them to the driver, said in flawless Greek, "Thank you very much, sir."

His face showed a flash of surprise, quickly followed by a dismissive shrug, as he turned around to grasp the wheel again.

Even though the evening was approaching, Selene could feel the day's heat still lingering in the air as soon as she stepped out of the car. Having retrieved her two duffel bags and her guitar case from the trunk, she walked back to the rear passenger side and gave the dented door a good shove with her hip, slamming it shut. The driver took this as his signal to speed away, leaving her alone at the depot. She drew a deep breath, threw her bags over her shoulders and made her way to the corner of the depot and up a narrow staircase sandwiched between two buildings. Her wide-brimmed sunhat rested low on her brow and her sunglasses were dark, but she didn't raise her head while crossing the church's courtyard. More than six years had passed since her last visit to the island, but her feet still knew exactly where to go.

The village of Oia was like a living time capsule – the local people's deep love and respect for the past had helped preserve it, and it had not changed drastically in many decades, in spite of heavy tourist traffic. The architecture displayed this fact in an obvious way. The traditional homes, known as cavehouses, still dotted Santorini's cliffsides, some of them providing shelter for over a century now. Carved into the volcanic rock itself, they sat layered so closely together that one resident's veranda often doubled as the roof of the house directly below it. Most of the cavehouses featured whitewashed exteriors, while others were painted with a variety of pastel shades, and the combination seemed to make the clustered abodes sparkle like diamonds in the bright Mediterranean light.

Switching the guitar case to her other hand, Selene turned left and wove her way through the throngs of people as she walked along the town's main pedestrian street. Constructed of large and slightly uneven pieces of white stone, the street guided her through the heart of the village, passing by jewellery shops, cafés, restaurants, galleries and various retailers that catered to the tourists. A cloudless sky greeted her, and the light breeze filled the air with the smell of the sea, but these familiar things did nothing to refresh her or offer comfort. Distracted for a moment, she lifted her head, glanced around and noticed that people were gathering all around her: young lovers on their honeymoon; older couples from the cruise ship anchored in the caldera; families crowding the patios of the larger hotels. They waited in anticipation, leaning against the railings or standing on rooftops and balconies, gathering together to share the same event. Selene peeked at her watch – it would be sunset in a few minutes. It was a perfect evening, but she had no interest in joining them. She just wanted to get herself inside.

As the iconic blue dome of St. George's Church drew near, Selene disappeared down another narrow set of stairs carved into the rock and coated with an uneven layer of concrete. The pathway snaked and dodged its way between the hotels and cavehouses, allowing access in some places to homes positioned nearly halfway down the escarpment. Where the stairs bent to the right, a short walkway darted to the left. Selene followed it and, when she reached its end a few feet later, found herself on a familiar veranda. An antique wrought-iron table set rested in its usual place, but the seat cushions had been stored away. The trough herb garden along the side desperately needed watering. The lapis-coloured window shutters and front door both looked a little weathered, but the whitewashed face of the old place glowed in the evening light. After pulling her keys from her purse, Selene stood, her feet frozen in place. She fumbled with them for a moment before raising her hand, sliding the key into the hole and then turning her wrist to hear the heavy lock click in the old wooden door.

The hinges let out an eerie creak as her free hand pushed the door open. The house's darkness and warmth beckoned her inside. Selene noticed the air smelled stale as she entered and dropped her bags just inside the main room. Her sandals squeaked on the cool tile floor as she pivoted in place before taking two slow steps toward the left wall, where she paused in front of a framed photograph. Her hand involuntarily lifted it off the rusted nail and her grasp tightened as she walked over to the front wall and sank onto the bench under the window. Her bright green eyes stared at it. A moment passed. Her tear broke the silence as it crashed down onto the glass. Her chest heaved and she swallowed hard as another tear fell on the frame, but her eyes barely blinked as they remained fixed on the photograph.

When Selene finally looked up, darkness filled the cavehouse – the last of the light passing through the shutter slats and the half-open door had disappeared. As if moving in slow motion, she stood and walked over to the light switch and flipped it on.

It all looked the same with everything in its place. After her foot nudged the door shut, Selene began to roam through the main room. Moving past the bookshelf, she glanced at the cookbooks, poetry anthologies and musty old novels, running her finger along their spines before looking away.

A walnut-framed loveseat lined the opposite wall and a well-worn rocking chair sat motionless next to it. She paused in the tiny, open-concept kitchen at the back of the main room to notice everything had been tucked away, save for the drying rack next to the sink. In front of her, at the very back, the two bedroom doors remained open. Selene's eyes never peered into the first bedroom; she headed straight for the smaller room on the right. When she flicked on the bedside table lamp, the dull bulb barely filled the shadows of the simple oak nightstand, the brass-framed bed and the ornately carved antique rolltop desk in the corner.

Her body, in its exhausted state, could not resist the lumpy old mattress, so she curled up on her side in the middle of it and stared again at the photograph. A friend had snapped it the last time she visited the island, when they were all together. Her family had just finished dinner on the veranda, celebrating with their neighbours because Selene had received word that Warner offered her band a contract. Her mother, Cora, sat next to her and grasped her hand, while her father, Frank, stood behind the ladies with a hand on each of their shoulders and a proud grin on his face. To outsiders, her parents might have seemed like an odd match. Frank possessed a naturally shy streak with more traditional values and a sense of propriety that, along with his Kiwi accent, often caused him to be mistaken for a Brit. Cora, on the other hand, had a reputation as a chatty social butterfly, influenced by the relaxed lifestyle that developed as she came of age in the Mediterranean during the early '70s. But to Selene it always seemed that, despite their differences, they perfectly complemented each other. Their romance began in the most unlikely of ways after a chance meeting at the opening party for Cora's gallery. As a child, Selene had always loved hearing her father recount that story. Selene secretly admired the romantic flair their marriage had maintained over the years and, as she grew up to see more of her friends' families split up, she valued her parents' bond as something rare and truly precious. But it was gone now, along with them, and the picture in her hand was all that remained. She pulled it in close and tight against her chest as her body began to tremble and tears finally burst from her eyes.

* * *

Selene woke with a groan the next morning and as her eyelids parted, she squinted, surprised by the light from the lamp she had left on all night. Sitting up slowly, she untwisted her body from its contorted sleeping position and noticed the dampness from night sweats triggered by unusual dreams already forgotten. She glanced at her watch – it was nearly eight o'clock – but she could tell that, despite sleeping for nearly eleven hours, she still seemed exhausted. Her family's last portrait had fallen to the floor at some point in the night so she felt relieved to see it still intact. She stretched and groaned some more as she walked into the main room, hung the frame back on the wall, opened the front window's shutters and pushed the glass outward on its hinge to let in the fresh air. Turning, her feet slowly retraced their path. Her hands stripped off her sweaty clothes and dropped each piece on the floor as she made her way to the bathroom. With the shower's knob turned to a barely warm temperature, she stepped under the water. Raising her arms to lean forward into the wall, she remained motionless as the steady flow trickled down her hunched shoulders and back.

Nearly ten minutes later, she emerged refreshed and alert, using a towel to dry her petite, athletic frame and dab some of the moisture out of her long black curls. Back in her bedroom, she slid a nude-coloured thong up her legs, followed by a pair of off-white linen pants and finished the outfit with a halter top that had a purple and brown paisley pattern. Standing in front of the mirror, she heard

Sunsets in Oia

a growl sound from deep within her as she rubbed a moisturizer into her olive-coloured arms, neck and face. Apparently, her hungry stomach needed some attention. Upon finding the fridge and kitchen cupboards empty, she realized she would have to go out shopping. After smoothing some tinted gloss on her lips and putting on her favourite pair of aviators, she grabbed her purse and a few of her mother's fabric shopping bags. She locked up the house, climbed the stairs to the street and made her way to the nearby supermarket. The shop was hardly 'super' though, even smaller than some North American-style gas station convenience stores, but it had everything an islander could need. Selene filled her basket with dried pasta, a can of olive oil, fresh oysters, frozen shrimp, bottles of fruit juice, a six-pack of Mythos beer, a loaf of bread and a large selection of locally grown vegetables and fruit. While waiting in a line for the cash register, she recalled how her mother brought her here twice weekly in the summers they had spent on the island, talking to her about food and teaching her how to shop for and cook traditional Greek cuisine.

A familiar voice calling her name pulled Selene out of her trance. Raising her head, her gaze landed on a short, plump woman standing before her wearing a surprised grin on her face. Selene had only a split second to recognize Sophia Kafieris' face before she wrapped Selene in a tight embrace, nearly knocking the basket out of her hand.

"My dear, I am surprised to see you! I did not know you came to town after the funeral. How are you? I hope you are good – you look so beautiful." The words spewed out of Sophia's mouth with such speed that Selene could barely keep up with her. She realized her ears were struggling to adjust to the local accent after not hearing it for so long.

"I've been quite knackered lately, but it's good to see you again," Selene said.

"It is lovely to see you too, dear. It feels like a long time."

In reality, Selene last saw Sophia only three weeks ago at her parents' funeral in Athens. She had known this woman her whole life – the Kafieris family lived just two levels up and one house over from her summer home and Sophia had been best friends with Cora for years. As a kid, Selene would run off and play with the three Kafieris children while the two mothers prepared feasts for their families to enjoy together at regular dinner parties. In fact, Selene spent more time with the Kafieris clan during her younger years than she did with her own cousins, who were scattered all over the world. All that changed, though, when things with her band took off and she started spending every summer on tour instead of on Santorini.

Selene had not noticed at the funeral but now thought Sophia looked as if she had aged fifteen years overnight. Her faded hair appeared nearly completely grey now, her neck showed early signs of a hump, and the bags under her eyes looked big enough to carry Selene's groceries. Yet, despite all this, a simple flash of her smile reminded Selene that Sophia once possessed an irresistible classic beauty and charm.

Sophia linked her arm with Selene's just then, pulling her out of the line and down an aisle, chattering away as she loaded things into her own basket. Nearly half an hour and an earful later, the women emerged from the market and began walking home together. As they reached the entrance to the large veranda in front of the Kafieris' home, Sophia drew Selene in for another hug and, as she pulled away, said, "You must come for dinner tonight."

Her expression suggested she would not let Selene decline the invitation, but when Selene hesitated for a moment, Sophia added, "You should not eat alone, dear. Come be with the family. I think of you as another daughter always."

Now Selene could not refuse. "All right, I'll come," she muttered, "but please don't fuss. I'm not ready for a big crowd right now."

"Of course, honey," Sophia said reassuringly. "Just family, I promise."

With a slight grin and a peck to the cheek, Sophia turned and disappeared into her home. *I can't believe I just agreed to go over for dinner. I just want to be alone.* Selene shook her head and stomped her way down the rest of the steps to her own door.

That evening, about an hour before sunset, Selene stood in her bedroom staring at her reflection in the mirror, wishing for an excuse to arise that would keep her from having to go to dinner. *No such luck; it's time to leave.* She slipped her feet into her sandals, locked the door behind her, and slowly made her way up the stairs to Sophia's home. As she crossed the veranda to the front door, the aroma of onions, oregano and grilled fish wafted out of the windows to greet her. She rapped against the door and immediately heard footsteps from within. However, the man who opened the door to her was not Sophia's husband, grumpy old Georgios. Standing nearly six feet tall, the handsome young man before her had a trim swimmer's body, broad shoulders and rich Mediterranean skin tanned dark by the sun. His square jaw and plump pink lips were framed by a slight five-o'clock shadow. Wavy, thick chestnut hair fell to just below his chin, with a few shorter pieces around his face to accent his cheekbones. He possessed the type of rugged sexiness that Selene associated with male models in European fashion magazines but the sight of his dark eyes and thick lashes inspired a barely audible gasp to escape from her lips.

"Is that really you, Nikos?"

"It is good to see you too, Selene." He had a strong and deep voice, and hearing him say her name made her weak in the knees for a moment. *Get a grip.*

Nikos took a step forward, wrapped his arm around her lower back and planted a kiss on her cheek.

"You look incredible," he whispered as he pulled away.

She felt herself blushing like a schoolgirl. Then Sophia's booming voice sounded from within.

"Is that Selene?" she shouted. "Bring her in, dear."

With his hand still on the small of her back, Nikos turned and guided her into the house. The place had not changed a bit since she last saw it at the age of nineteen, except for several new pieces of art displayed on the walls. Selene paused to admire each of them – a trio of small canvases depicting Santorini scenes in the classic local style, a charcoal portrait of Georgios, and a hauntingly dark oil painting of a gothic cathedral. Only after admiring the collection did she notice they all had the same initials, N.K., in the corner.

"Is this your work?" she asked as she turned to him.

"Yes," he said, a broad grin on his face, "I did these years ago when studying in Athens. They are some of the only ones I never sold."

"Of course you don't sell them," shouted Sophia as she walked over to them. "You owed us something to look at after we paid for all those art classes." With a crooked grin on her face, Sophia gave her son a light tap on the cheek and added, "Now come make yourself useful and carry the food out to the table."

He took a platter of red snapper with stuffed tomatoes and a large bowl of horiatiki salad from the counter and carried them outside to the veranda. As Sophia handed the plates and cutlery to Selene, Georgios slowly emerged from the bedroom. A shock hit Selene as she saw his diminished state. He shuffled along with the aid of a cane, clearly favouring one leg; his poor balance and the curve of his neck forced him to stare at his feet as he moved; and his weathered face now had a significant droop on one side. *Oh great, now he has more to be grumpy about.* Still, she felt a bit sad to see him in such condition considering he was only sixty-four. He shot her a quick glare when he noticed her watching him, so she made an abrupt turn and carried the dishes outside.

"How was your birthday last week?" she asked as she joined Nikos on the veranda.

"You remembered."

"Of course. Because of you, there was always a big party to start our summers here."

"It was quiet this year. No big party."

"But it's the last year of your twenties," she pointed out. "You should have done something wild."

"My birthday… always with your family for so long. It feels strange this year. I did not want to party."

Selene nodded and said nothing as Nikos helped her set the table, but a slight smile spread across her face. *His English still isn't perfect, but there's something so soothing about his voice.* Georgios slowly made his way over and eased into the chair at the head of the table. Sophia placed a bottle of Boutari wine and four tumblers on the table and took her place in the chair opposite her husband. As they began to eat, the pounding sound of gunfire rang out from above, with the echo of a violin softly playing between each explosion. The noise did not alarm them, though, because it announced the arrival of a wedding party at a nearby church for a traditional ceremony.

"I wonder did they manage to scare away the

bride," Georgios mumbled, a common joke that still drew laughter from all of them.

After a pause, Selene raised her gaze from her plate to look across at Nikos.

"You know, I was surprised to see you here tonight. Your mum didn't mention you'd be joining us and the last I heard, you were still living in Athens."

"I know; the look on your face at the door ... like you see a ghost," he replied with a smile. "She calls me this morning to say she saw you at the market and, when she mentioned dinner, I had to come see you again."

"You flew down for dinner to see me?"

"No," he laughed. "I live in town now." He looked with soft eyes to his father. "When father had his stroke last year, he could not teach anymore but he convinced the administration to hire me for his class. It was a good move. Things in Athens were getting hard and Antonia closed the gallery a few months after I come here."

"So you left your life as an artist to become a school teacher. I'm shocked."

"I still paint at my house in my own time and my cousin in Fira is selling my work in his shop," he revealed. "But I love the school now. And it is good I am so close now to help at home. I could not leave my mother alone to deal with this old guy."

He flashed his father a smile and slapped his knee but Georgios did not look amused at being the butt of Nikos' joke. Instead, he pulled his worry beads from his pocket and began to rub them as a hush fell over the table.

"Do you miss Athens at all?" Selene asked, breaking the silence after a moment.

"Sometimes, yes," he admitted. "But I saw the gallery will close soon and things were not good for me in other ways. It was time to go."

"You know, he was engaged back there," Sophia added, butting into the conversation.

"Really?" Selene glanced over to Sophia and back at him.

"Mama!" Nikos tried to protest the subject but Sophia only waved her hand dismissively at him and continued to gossip.

"She was pregnant, too, but then she... Ah, what is the word for this? For losing the baby..."

"A miscarriage," Selene offered.

"Yes," Sophia nodded. "It was hard on them. Nikos got obsessed with work but Eleni got very depressed. Then she runs off with her boss, they have an affair and broke my Nikos' heart, so he came back here."

The sound of Nikos tossing his fork down on his plate startled the women and Selene watched as he shot his mother a glare. His face was flushed and she could tell he was embarrassed, so she tried to offer him some comfort.

"This may not mean much to you now, Nikos, but I think you deserve better than someone who would treat you that way. I understand what you're going through." She offered him a soft, sweet smile that seemed to cause the anger on his face to melt away.

"What about you, Selene? How is your love life?" Sophia inquired. "Your mother told me a while ago you are dating some famous footballer."

"Ah yes, Andrew," she nodded. "We broke up six months ago."

"Why?"

"Turns out he was cheating on me with a dancer, and I found out about it through the press. I dumped him, and he ran off with her."

Sophia was shocked. "Oh, that is awful."

"He did not deserve you," Nikos said.

"No, he didn't," she sighed. "You see: both of us deserved better. And I guess you could say now we're both damaged goods because of it. But at least we can commiserate with each other."

She dipped her head to the side and flashed him a crooked smile, which he returned before the four of them reverted their attention to the food.

When the sky began to darken and a cool breeze

put a chill in the air, Sophia cleared the table and the foursome went inside for baklava and coffee. Nikos handed Selene her cup and joined her on the sofa facing his art. They sipped in silence for a moment before he turned to her and softly said, "I'm very sorry I did not go to Athens with my mother to be there for you. One of us had to stay home with father. I am sorry for what happened to them." He rested his hand on her knee to comfort her.

"Please," she said, with polite dismissiveness. "It's fine. You don't have to apologize, Nikos." He seemed to take the hint as she changed the subject. "These are actually the first pieces of your work I've seen. They're wonderful. I especially like Georgios' portrait. You really captured him."

"It's too honest," grumbled Georgios from his seat in the corner.

"Actually, I think it's quite endearing," she countered rather forcefully, putting the old man in his place in a way that brought a smile to Nikos' face. "I wish I had the talent to give my family a gift like that."

As soon as the words slipped through her lips, she felt a pang of regret, realizing she no longer had a family to whom she could offer such a gift. She dropped her head to stare into her coffee cup, trying to fight the tears that so desperately wanted to escape from her eyes.

"I think you did already," Nikos suggested. "They loved your music and were very proud of you, I'm sure."

Without raising her head, Selene faked half a smile to acknowledge his effort, but she was barely holding it together. Georgios seemed not to notice.

"Such a shame, a tragic end. But foolish. What were they doing there so close to the rioting? Foolish, I say."

"Papa!" Nikos shot his father a look to get him to stop, but it was of no use.

"And why were there so many cameras? It was all over the news," he continued. "I did not have to go to the funeral – I could watch from here. No respect, I say, those journalists."

Georgios didn't realize that those cameras were there for Selene. As soon as the paparazzi caught wind of the news, they had followed her from New Zealand to Greece, haunting her every step of the way to the funeral. She could still hear the sound of their camera shutters clicking rapidly as they attempted to capture a shot of the famous, grieving daughter.

Georgios' words and the sounds in her head proved too much. She stood up abruptly and her trembling hands abandoned her coffee to the table.

Her eyes welled up as she looked to Sophia and, with a shaky voice, declared, "I can't do this." Then she looked down at Nikos and whispered, "I'm sorry," as she turned and fled from their house.

* * *

Nikos watched as Sophia stepped over to her husband and gave him a swift smack to the back of the head.

"Now look what you've done!" she yelled at him in Greek. Her intense glare and reddened face caused him to hang his head in shame. She turned to her son and half shouted, "What should we do? Where would she run to?"

A quiet pause filled the air as Nikos paced about the room while his mother stared at him. "I think I know," he said finally, grabbing the blanket off the back of the sofa as he rushed out the door.

* * *

Selene found her favourite place and sat herself atop a large, flat piece of rock jutting out from the cliffside twenty metres below the village. She sat near its edge with her back to the island as she stared out at the shadowy waters of the caldera.

Her hair blew wildly in the evening breeze and her shoulders quivered as she finally cried. Her sobs and the whirling wind masked the sound of approaching footsteps, but she realized she wasn't alone when she heard Nikos softly calling her name from behind the rock. Startled, she wiped her eyes before turning to him.

"What are you doing here?"

"I thought you might want to talk."

"No, I don't," she said sternly.

"Okay," he uttered as he sat down to her right. He wrapped the blanket around her shoulders and the sweet gesture caused her face to soften. They sat in silence for a long time staring out at the sea.

"I can't believe this is happening to me," she murmured. "It's all so surreal. I feel orphaned and homeless at the same time. I hate this."

Without speaking, Nikos wrapped his arm around her and the silent comfort was the first bit of genuine reassurance she had felt in weeks. She leaned into his shoulder and let herself weep in his presence. He chastely kissed the top of her head and held her tightly in his strong arms, and the warmth of his body on that cool night seemed to have some sort of healing properties. After only a couple of minutes, she didn't feel like crying anymore. Instead, her thoughts shifted to how abruptly she had run

Sunsets in Oia

out on his family and she felt embarrassed by her behaviour. She blotted her face with the corner of the blanket and looked up at him.

"I hope your parents aren't mad that I ran out of there."

"Don't worry. They understand."

"How did you find me?"

"I knew you would be here."

Selene shot him a look of surprise. "What?"

"You have not changed all that much since we were kids," he explained, smiling down at her. "When you had a fight with your parents or feel frustrated, you ran down here to escape. This was your favourite spot – do you remember?"

She laughed at herself a bit upon hearing this as those memories returned. "That was so long ago. How did you remember that?"

"It has been many years, yes, but I still know you better than you think."

"Am I really that predictable?"

"Don't worry," he said playfully. "I think it is a good thing."

Selene's mouth parted into a smile and they shared a quick laugh together before she returned her head to his shoulder and stared up at the stars. After a few minutes of companionable silence between them, with the distant sound of the crashing waves hitting the rocks below, Nikos turned his head to her and spoke again.

"I remember all of it, you know. All the summers our families spent together."

"That's exactly my problem now: being here only reminds me of them," she said, her voice shaking as she tried to control the impulse to cry again. "I feel like an incomplete puzzle with just the right pieces missing to prevent me from seeing the picture clearly. And no matter what I do, I can't get those pieces back."

Nikos placed his finger under her chin so she would look at him. "I know you feel awful now, but try to realize, you are not as alone as you think."

His dark eyes seemed to glow in the moonlight as he looked at her, and his unwavering gaze sent a rush of heat through her body that, against the sea breeze, caused her to tremble.

"Come, you are cold," he motioned as he misread her body's movement. "Let me take you home."

She nodded and they stood up together. With his arm still around her shoulder, they slowly made their way up the steps to her front door. Upon reaching it, she turned and handed the blanket back to him.

"Thank you, Nikos," she said with great sincerity. "I'm glad you were here."

"Don't worry, Selene. You will be all right, I

promise." With that, he pulled her in for a tight hug, stroking her arm as he released her, and then wished her a good night.

* * *

Nikos walked up the steps and slipped back into his parents' house to bid them good night. Georgios had not budged from the chair in the corner while Sophia stood in the kitchen, washing the dishes from dinner.

"Did you find her?" she asked in her native tongue when Nikos walked in.

"Yes. She was down sitting on her favourite rock. We talked and she feels better now. I just walked her home."

"You be careful with that girl, son."

"What do you mean?"

"I saw that look in your eyes tonight," she said as she tossed the dish towel over her shoulder and walked over to him. "I know you still like her. I'm your mother – I can tell."

"Mama!" Nikos stared at his feet as Sophia reached up and lovingly tucked a piece of his hair behind his ear.

"Just remember: she is very fragile right now. We all have to take care of her."

"She's a good woman," Georgios piped in. "You deserve someone like her. Don't be so shy like you were as a boy."

Sophia shushed her husband and lightly swatted him with the dish towel.

"My god! Will you two stop?" Nikos insisted. "I know what I'm doing."

Smiling, he kissed his parents on their foreheads, said good night and walked out of the house. Nikos made his way along the pedestrian street until it intersected with the main road, which he followed to the outskirts of the village until it met with the edge of neighbouring Finikia. He walked swiftly against the cool evening breeze while thinking about the evening's events and the flurry of feelings now confronting him. He realized it would be insensitive to rush things with Selene and, after the events of the previous year, he questioned if he was even ready to act on his enduring attraction to her. *Can I handle this again after what went down with Eleni? I don't know. Still, this is Selene. After all these years, here she is again. I can't ignore that. One day at a time, man, just one day at a time.*

Nikos walked up a long driveway to his home, a run-down, old house on the edge of a farm that the previous owners had abandoned for a larger property down the road. When Nikos returned to the island, he had lived with his parents for a few months while looking for a new place and had only moved into the farmhouse a few months earlier after doing extensive renovations to the interior. The summer heat had arrived early that year so his work on the exterior of the house had to wait. The single-storey dwelling did not offer much more room than some of Oia's larger cavehouses, but he liked that it sat in a peaceful location away from the tourist action, offered plenty of natural light through large windows and had a small vegetable garden in the side lot.

He unlocked the door and entered the house, where dark shadows filled the front rooms. Flicking on the hall light, Nikos kicked off his shoes near the door and walked through the living room. Devoid of much furniture, it only featured a worn leather lounge chair, floor lamp and television. An abundance of art supplies and a few belongings still piled in unopened boxes crowded the opposite corner. Nikos walked past them to the door along the back wall, which led to his bedroom. Exhausted, he stripped down to his underwear, abandoning his clothes on the floor, and collapsed into his bed.

* * *

Try as she might, Selene couldn't fall asleep that night. Deep in the cave, alone in her bed, blackness surrounded her. The windowless room, hidden from all traces of light, was only penetrated by the distant whistling of the wind as it sped across the open sea and pushed against the island. To her, it sounded like the eerie whisper of an unseen spirit floating from room to room, seeking contact with the land of the living that it left behind. She peered up at the dimpled, imperfect ceiling, straining her eyes while strange shapes took form above her. The bumps and divots appeared as bottomless black eyes, a lidless gaze fixed on her. Their unflinching stare made her feel anxious. A plethora of questions flooded her thoughts, drowning all certainties she once considered invincible.

How am I ever going to bounce back from this? Where do I belong now? And what am I doing back here? This place may look the same in the light of day but now it's as if I'm stuck in a dark, black hole in the ground. This room's making me claustrophobic and the walls smell like that funeral home -- musty, stale, lingering death. I've gone from putting my parents to rest to tucking myself into a tomb. What the hell was I thinking when I came down here? I'm a fool for thinking it would feel the same. Just when I thought things couldn't get worse, now the one place that always gave me peace

Sunsets in Oia

is torturing and taunting me. I've gotta get out of here.

Selene rolled over and buried her face in the pillow, but the knowledge that the black eyes above were glaring down her neck kept her awake for hours.

Chapter Two

At eleven o'clock the following day, Selene was sitting on the veranda enjoying a pot of tea and watching the hot morning sun burn off the mist that hung over the water when Nikos appeared. His visit caught her off guard but her face broke into a broad smile when he pulled his hand from behind his back and presented her with a bouquet of purple and yellow crocus flowers.

"I thought these would make you feel better," he said as he handed them to her and she buried her nose in them to inhale their sweet scent. Selene gestured to him to join her for tea and he made himself comfortable at the table. She slipped into the house, filled a turquoise clay vase with water and placed the flowers on the small table next to the kitchen before returning to Nikos with a ceramic mug.

An hour and another pot of tea later, the conversation was flowing effortlessly and Selene felt relaxed for the first time in weeks. Once they emptied the pot, Nikos suggested, "I think it would be good for you to go out, enjoy yourself. I know Uncle Pavlo would be glad to see you again. You always liked to eat at his restaurant. We should go for lunch."

She considered her empty stomach and the good company. "All right, but I can't stay too long. I have an appointment at three."

When he nodded without inquiring about the appointment, she felt relieved – she had a feeling he would not approve of her plan. They carried the dishes indoors and then walked to the other side of Oia until they reached Pavlo's restaurant, Bougainvillea. Two flourishing vines framed the entrance, displaying their crimson petals and white flowers in full bloom – the very blossoms that inspired the place's name. Inside, the ground level looked much as Selene remembered: three rows of tables filled the floor, with a fourth row of booths on the far right wall, leading to the bar and kitchen at the back. Nikos said a few but friendly quick words to the host, as if he had known the young man for years, and Selene noticed that there was something vaguely familiar about him. He led them up the stairs, and Selene saw the upstairs section had changed drastically. The second level was once half the size and used for large parties but a major renovation had obviously occurred since her last visit. Pavlo had knocked down part of the back wall, installed sliding glass doors and turned the unused rooftop into an open-air patio dining space. Thick strips of fabric in baby blue and sea-foam green, woven over and under wooden beams to look like waves, offered some cover, supported by white stucco-covered columns draped with more bougainvillea plants in three different colours. Their fragrance and bright hues brought back so many wonderful memories of times spent dining there with her family, which made Selene smile as they walked out to the patio.

The host seated them at a small table near the rear but they hardly had time to get comfortable before Pavlo appeared with a giant, yellow-toothed grin on his round face. He gave each of them a sloppy kiss on both cheeks – a trait for which he was rather infamous – and told them that their lunch would be on the house in honour of Selene's special visit.

"Look at you, my dear," he bellowed while

pinching her chin between his thick, rough thumb and finger. "You stay away too long. I will get you some food and come sit with you."

As Pavlo disappeared inside, the host returned, setting their table with white and blue plates, cutlery and a clipping of fragrant white jasmine in a stumpy vase. As the young man turned away again, Selene turned to Nikos, gesturing to the host, and asked, "Do I know him? He looks familiar."

"I should hope so," replied Nikos with a chuckle. "You did not recognize my cousin? That is Pavlo's son, Stefanos."

"My god," Selene gasped, "but he was just a kid!"

"You have been away a long time," he reminded her. "Kids tend to grow up."

Father and son returned swiftly with trays of fresh bread and oil, calamari, souvlaki, and fava beans as well as a pitcher of beer and the four of them gorged themselves on the meal, with Stefanos getting up intermittently to check on the other patrons downstairs. As the afternoon wore on, Pavlo broke out the Ouzo and then revealed he had a surprise for Selene. She flashed him a puzzled look and he fled inside for a moment, returning with Stefanos and another employee, Spiro, each of them carrying musical instruments.

"What's going on?" she asked Nikos.

"Just wait."

The three men positioned themselves on a short platform in the front corner of the patio and broke into song, giving Selene and Nikos a private performance of traditional Greek folk tunes. The whole experience, its delicious food, friendly company and vibrant music, reinvigorated Selene and served as a welcome distraction from the regrettable events that had recently come to dominate her life.

"Hey Pavlo, play something Selene can sing with you," Nikos suddenly shouted out while giving Selene an encouraging look.

"Yes, yes!" Pavlo proclaimed as he waved her over to them. "Let us hear your beautiful voice, my dear."

She couldn't do it. Something deep inside stopped her; an uncontrollable feeling told her to remain mute. Selene could see the disappointment on Nikos' face when he realized she would decline, but she still felt like an excuse was needed. Glancing down at her wrist, her watch told her it was a good time to leave.

"I'm sorry," she said with as much sincerity as she could muster, "but I have to go." She stood, looked down at Nikos and gripped his right hand as it rested on the table. "I'm running late for that appointment, but thank you for this." Before he could respond, she turned to the other men, shouted out, "Next time, guys," and hustled out of the restaurant.

I haven't actually lied to Nikos about running late. Their lunch had gone on so long she only had a few minutes to get across town again, so her feet picked up the pace to jog along the pedestrian street, dodging the oncoming tourists blocking her path. It felt good to run.

By the time she reached her destination, Selene's throat had gone dry, her chest felt tight and her feet throbbed from having run in flimsy sandals. Pausing for a moment with her hands resting on her hips, trying to catch her breath, she felt a slight hesitation about entering the estate agent's office in front of her. The small building was likely a former private residence itself but had gone through considerable renovations to convert it into a place of business. Two large display windows dominated the facade and posters nearly completely covered them to advertise local properties for sale or rent. A narrow wooden door, painted a burnt red colour resembling the volcanic earth that covered much of the island, stood sandwiched between the windows. Selene turned the squeaky antique iron knob and pushed the door in. She was greeted by a rush of cold air-conditioned air and the sound of fingernails tapping on keyboards and soft voices chattering on the phones. Inside, a small receptionist's desk sat near the entrance on the left while a manager's office filled most of the remaining space on that wall. Three work stations occupied the right side of the room. Employees sat behind the identical desks, with two chairs placed in front of them for clients.

Speaking in Greek, Selene informed the receptionist she was there to meet a sales agent and was then directed to the middle desk on the right side of the office. Greeting the young woman with a firm handshake and introducing herself by her first name, Selene withdrew a portfolio from her bag that contained the deed and other documents connected to the house. She handed it to the woman and quickly sat down to get to business.

As the agent opened the folder and began looking over the papers, Selene stared at the items on her desk: a small potted plant, a couple of framed photographs, a stack of pens in a plastic holder, all cluttering the space around her Mac desktop computer. Just as Selene's eyes fell on the nameplate in front of her, the agent's voice caught her attention.

"Wait – this deed says Doherty. You're Selene Doherty?"

She nodded her head and the agent flashed her a giant smile.

"It's me, Vicky."

Selene glanced down at the nameplate again

— Viktoria Karnezi. *Could this really be the chubby, shy girl who used to play with me and the Kafieris kids all those years ago?*

It certainly didn't look like her; the woman sitting before her was tall and slender, with perky breasts, big white teeth and blonde streaks in her long, thick hair that had been ironed flat. But when Selene noticed the pointy nose supporting her glasses and the beady eyes behind them, she knew they were one and the same.

"I'm so sorry, Vicky," she started. "I didn't recognize you."

"Me neither," she replied excitedly. "I had no idea you were my next appointment. How wonderful. I didn't know you were still on the island… but you've decided to sell, I see…" Vicky's voice trailed off as she looked again at the deed and when she noticed the address she frowned. "But this is your parents' house."

"It was their place," Selene corrected her, "but it was transferred to my name when they died last month."

"Died! Both of them?"

"You didn't know? It was all over the news."

"I had no idea. I was backpacking through South America with my fiancé this last month. We just returned a week ago. Selene, I am so sorry.

What happened?"

Selene bowed her head, taking in a deep breath.

"It's not something I really want to discuss here."

Vicky nodded solemnly, sighed and then stood up. "Come," she said, "let's go get a coffee and talk."

She shouted to her boss in the back office that she was stepping out for a bit and guided Selene back out the front door.

The hot afternoon sun made them squint as they turned left down the street, and Vicky linked her arm with Selene's as they walked in silence. The women reached a small café a few doors down and Vicky ordered a sweet frappé for each of them. Climbing the narrow set of stairs at the back, they found their way to a tiny rooftop patio and made themselves comfortable at a secluded table. Selene didn't know how to start so she was glad when Vicky spoke first.

"I remember your parents clearly... such wonderful people. We were all so close back then. I know this is hard for you. You see, I lost my father last year to cancer. But you can't hold it all inside. You must talk about it, Selene."

"He died of a disease, Vicky. My parents were taken from me. It's not the same." Selene wasn't sure why she was being so defensive, perhaps she resented the comparison, but she knew that Vicky

Sunsets in Oia

was right about bottling up her feelings.

"What do you mean they were taken?"

"When you were off backpacking, did you not hear about how bad the riots were getting in Athens?"

"There was a bit in the news about the big marches last month and some violence, but most of the coverage I saw was in Spanish, so I didn't follow things closely."

Selene nodded and took a deep breath. This would be the first time she would share the story that the government told her about how her parents were killed.

"It was May 5, the evening of the nationwide strike, and things were quickly getting out of control in the square."

She paused for a moment and could feel a lump forming in her throat, but Vicky didn't say anything and she was grateful for her silence.

"Young protesters took advantage of the peaceful strike and started tossing Molotov cocktails through the windows of banks, government offices and store-fronts. One smashed through the window of a shop closed for renovations. The flames ignited a stack of paint cans and chemicals piled against the wall. The explosion wasn't planned and caught my parents as they were running by.

"The force of it knocked out part of the wall. My father was buried alive by the rubble. Mum was badly wounded, and the crowd nearby started to panic. She ended up being trampled to death."

When Selene looked back up at Vicky through teary eyes, she saw that her old friend was crying too. Her mouth parted but no words escaped. The women sat in silence for many minutes and Vicky held tightly onto Selene's hand as she dropped her head and let herself feel the loss. Selene was glad to have Vicky's quiet but firm support.

"I had just landed in Auckland," she continued. "I'd been on tour for nearly two months with the band and we only had a few shows left back at home in New Zealand. I was walking through the lobby of the airport when I got the call…" Her voice trailed off, her throat gone dry with the telling, so she just started sipping her coffee again. A few more minutes of silence passed.

"After the funeral, I found out they had willed the Oia cavehouse to me. They knew it had always been my favourite place. But when I came down a few days ago I realized I couldn't be here anymore – not without them. It's just not the same. So I've decided to sell it; I need your help to get rid of it as fast as possible. I can't be in it anymore."

"Are you sure this is what you want to do?"

Sunsets in Oia

Vicky asked.

"I have to." Her voice was quivering and quiet. In her mind, Selene wasn't actually sure if it was the right course, but she couldn't bear the alternative: owning a home that would always remind her of the wonderful times she shared with her family there and of the horrific circumstances that arose that led to it being left to her. She wanted to forget it all, the love her parents gave to her and the pain of loss that remained. *There's only so much one heart can take before it breaks forever.*

Vicky offered Selene a simple nod, acknowledging she would respect her grieving friend's wishes.

"I'll take care of it."

"Thank you, Vicky. I'm glad it's you handling this for me. No one else would understand quite like you."

* * *

Three days had passed since Selene met with Vicky and she now faced a mix of emotions: relief, frustration, anxiety and a twinge of regret, the latter which she was not yet willing to acknowledge. Considering what she was trying to achieve, selling the cavehouse to help her move on, it wasn't going to be easy in the current troubled and uncertain economic times. *It won't be like ripping off a Band-Aid; more like bouncing back from a head-on car wreck.*

As she sat on her favourite rock below the village late that afternoon listening to the sea, her cell phone rang and the wreck quickly turned into a multi-car pile-up.

"Selene, it's Roger."

That bastard. What does he want now?

This was his third call to her since the funeral and she had let the first two go to voicemail. *I can't ignore him anymore.*

Roger Carmichael was the band's manager, a ruthlessly efficient man who had managed to turn Kauri Spirit into a well-oiled, money-making machine, thus changing Selene's love of playing music into an actual job, something of a chore of late. The reality had become increasingly obvious during the recent tour.

"What is it, Roger?" she sighed.

"Just thought I'd ring you up to see how you're managing, love."

Always playing nice with an ulterior motive; that's my manager.

"Well, let's see: my family is dead and I'm stuck in a house that is basically a shrine to their memories and now you're on the line again for god-knows-what reason. Otherwise, I'm just peachy. And you?"

"Don't get smart with me, girl," he ordered. "I'm here working for you, remember? And you've been AWOL a month now. You haven't even called your boys or me once. Do I need to remind you that you have responsibilities here? You skipped out on seven dates in your own country. This is your home base I'm talking about. You've left me to clean up the mess. Now, I'm sorry for what happened, love, but those contracts still stand. When are you coming back? And it better be soon."

Selene stood on the cliff's edge, furious with Roger's insensitivity and money-grubbing intentions.

"Look, Roger, you may be good at your job but you've got your head stuck way up your ass right now. I'll come home when I'm damn good and ready. But don't hold your breath. You may end up as dead as my parents!"

She hung up and nearly threw her phone down to smash it on the cliffside but caught herself, plopping back down on her rock. She didn't budge until the stars and crescent moon were the only lights in the night sky.

Selene barely slept that night, haunted by her confrontation with Roger and chastising herself for the spontaneously immature and selfish way she had behaved. Part of her, the part still searching for a way to move past everything, knew her manager was right about certain things, though she would never admit that to him. The next morning, Selene paced and dragged around the house, mumbling to herself as she tried to sort through her feelings of confusion and resentment. As she struggled to eat her light breakfast of yogurt with honey and fruit, she began to wonder if Vicky was right. *Do I really just need an outlet, a way to express myself and all the thoughts swirling in my head?*

This internal question kept poking and prodding at her psyche until she instinctively reached for her guitar case. She carried it out to the veranda, sat down in one of the chairs and slowly flipped the latches open. The familiar clicking sound sent a slight chill down her spine, and as she pushed back the hard cover to reveal the polished form of her beloved Fender acoustic, Selene had to pause for a moment before she had the strength to pull it from its resting place. It had been a Sweet 16 birthday gift from her parents and had always been her favourite of all of her guitars. She always went back to it when composing something new. As she lifted it out and placed it on her knee, its weight and smooth finish felt strangely familiar and yet confusingly foreign.

Selene took her time plucking each string to tune the instrument. Nearly twenty minutes passed

Sunsets in Oia

before she felt ready to strike the first chord of a song. *Just start slowly, I can do this. I may not be able to go back in time, but dwelling in all this negativity and giving into this weak lonely girl state isn't helping. I just have to focus. Just me and my guitar. This is what I do best.*

No matter how hard Selene focused her fragile mind, her body would not comply. She started with the introduction to "Lazy Man," a pounding rock anthem that had become the band's latest hit, but she could barely control the strings long enough to get to the opening verse. Shaking out her fingers, she next attempted to play the coincidentally titled, "Nothing's Easy When You're Gone," the second single from their first album, which remained the band's most popular tune. Still she stumbled constantly and gave up halfway through. She could normally perform it with her eyes closed. *Why is this so hard?* Selene made a last effort with "Steady," an ironic choice, she realized, because it seemed to inspire a tremble in her limbs that quickly became uncontrollable. An hour later, her patience expired, she resorted to playing familiar cover songs but could not get her mind and body to obey her wishes.

Frustrated and defeated, she returned her guitar to its case and was retreating inside when she heard her phone ring. "That better not be Roger again," she mumbled as she reached for it. Glancing at the screen, the Caller-ID told her it was Nikos, and the sight of his name helped her to muster a smile.

"Well, this is certainly a surprise," she said as she put the phone to her ear.

"And, judging by your tone, it is not a welcomed one," he replied.

How is it that he can see right through me, even if all he has to go on is the sound of my voice?

"Sorry, just having a rough couple of days, is all."

"Oh really… rougher than usual?" His sarcastic tone surprised her; he usually managed to poke fun at her while still remaining sensitive.

"Yes, if you must know. I heard from my manager yesterday and we got into it. He's so focused on the band and the leftover tour dates and insisted that I come home. It came off as rude and upsetting, especially since that's the last thing on my mind right now. But he still managed to make me feel guilty for being here. So I've been trying to play some bits on my guitar but it's as if I'd never held it before."

"Wow! Is that all? And I thought it might be something serious."

He's trying to cheer me up and flirt at the same time. Well, two can play that game.

"And I suppose you're calling with some bit of profound news or sensible advice, am I right?" she asked. "Nikos to the rescue."

They laughed at the absurdity of the conversation, and Selene started to realize that, of all the people still in her life, he somehow knew how to lift her up with just a few simple words – a quality that astounded and delighted her. *Why him of all people?*

"I am serious now," he continued in a more subdued tone. "What is wrong over there? Why can't you play?"

"I'm not quite sure really," she admitted. "It all sounds so muddled in my head and my hands can't make sense of it and every note I hit sounds flat and lifeless… It's as if I've forgotten how to do what I do best and that's a rather disturbing notion."

A silence on the other end lingered for a moment and lasted just long enough for Selene to think they had been disconnected.

"I think you may be trying too hard."

"Really… is that all?"

"I mean this, Selene," he said. "You go through so much and you want so badly for it to just go away. You of all people know music doesn't work that way."

"And what do you know about that?" She was surprised she was being so defiant.

"It sounds to me that you are thinking too much," he said with a soft voice. "You know you have to let yourself feel it first. Once you are honest with yourself, your fingers… they will follow."

How could I have been so foolish? He's right: it's not something I can force. She swallowed hard to regain her voice and then let out a sigh.

"Thanks, Nikos. I needed to hear that," she said softly and then paused. "How is it that you know so much?"

"I know you – remember?"

Selene let out an uneasy laugh, amazed that a man she had been apart from for so long still managed to see her so clearly.

"I am thinking maybe you need another distraction," he suggested.

"Are you proposing something?"

"A proposal, no," he quipped. "But I thought we could start with a date."

Was he just making a joke again, or is he being serious? Slightly stunned, her throat suddenly ran as dry as desert wasteland while her brain went into overdrive.

"Really?" Selene managed to choke out the word.

"I know the timing isn't great, but…"

"You're right, it's not, but I think I can manage," she said slowly.

"Is that a 'yes?'" he asked with a laugh.

"That's a 'sort-of yes.' But to be honest, Nikos, I'm not sure if a distraction is what I need right now. In fact, I feel more like a drink."

There was a pause on the other end for a moment. "I think I can work with that. I'll pick you up on Saturday at six."

Before she could respond to accept his suggestion, Nikos hung up.

Hmm, I didn't see that coming after all these years. A date with Nikos – what could this mean? I'm going to have to be careful about this.

After setting down her phone, Selene became nervous about making a date with Nikos. *I don't think I can wait until Saturday for that drink.* She picked up her phone and called Vicky and the two of them made plans to drive into Fira that evening for a night of drinking and dancing.

Later that evening, Selene felt excited as she dressed herself in a red strapless top, black miniskirt and gold-coloured, knee-high stiletto boots. *It'll be nice to get out of the house to relax and just hang out.* At 11 p.m., she met Vicky along the main road next to St. George's Church to drive to the capital.

"You look great," Vicky said as Selene hopped into the car.

"Thanks. You do too. I love the tribal pattern in that dress."

"Oh, thanks. I bought it in Buenos Aires with Gabriel."

After the short drive, Vicky parked the car in downtown Fira and the ladies walked along the street, trying to decide where to go. Even though it was early, the clubs were already getting busy with lines starting to form outside some of them. Thankfully, Vicky spotted her friend Andreas as they approached Koo Club and he welcomed them inside.

"Andreas, I'd like you to meet an old friend of mine –"

"Selene Doherty," he said as he reached out and kissed her hand. "You are very welcome here. I'm a big fan. Come, ladies, I will give you a VIP table."

This is what I love about this island: away from my scene, I can disappear in a crowd. The few people who do recognize me are always so nice.

Andreas led them through the club to the outdoor party area, which was already half full with patrons drinking, relaxing and dancing under the palm trees. Mere moments after they sat down at a comfy lounge area overlooking the dance floor, a waiter arrived with a bottle of champagne, saying it was a treat from Andreas. Selene poured each of them a glass and, turning to Vicky, said, "To old friends and a much-needed girls' night out."

Several glasses of champagne and a couple of martinis later, Selene and Vicky laughed and joked with each other while recalling old times, thoroughly enjoying the chance to catch up. The crowd below them had come alive, dancing up a storm as the DJ blasted electronic and dance tunes over the speakers.

"There are a lot of good-looking people here tonight," Selene pointed out as she sipped the last of her cocktail.

"I see the men... They keep looking up at us," Vicky added, leaning toward her. "I think they're checking you out."

"Well, maybe we should go down and join them? Come on, let's dance."

Vicky knocked back the last of her drink and Selene led her down the few steps into the crowd. A remixed version of Artie Cabrera and Lisa Pure's "Rain Falls" rang out around them as they began to groove to the beat. About a half hour later, Vicky disappeared briefly to go to the bathroom and Selene continued to dance with the people around her, allowing the heavy bass beats to suppress all of the negative thoughts occupying her mind. As the crowd shifted around and bodies rubbed up against each other, she closed her eyes for a moment and was lost to the frenzy. When her eyes opened again, she noticed that two men were closing in around her.

"You're that singer, Selene, right?" the tall one in the green shirt asked as he slipped his arm around her waist. "You're hot. Dance with me."

"Not interested," she shouted out over the music and turned away, only to have her path blocked by his friend, who had greasy hair and giant biceps. She could smell the booze on them as they moved in closer. Despite their intoxication, she sensed right away they were the aggressive type.

"Come on, babe. Party with us." He moved in, gripped her rear and started grinding against her as the other one held her by the shoulders.

"Get off me," she shouted and shoved his sweaty chest, but he persisted. Just as Vicky reappeared, the buff tourist moved in on Selene again and tried to kiss her as his friend blocked her escape.

I don't think so! Selene gripped the man's shoulder and drove her knee into his groin with the full force of her body, which sent him keeling over as he gripped his throbbing twins. The man in green grabbed her by the arm and called her a bitch as he spun her around. She saw his swinging arm heading toward her to slap her face, but she blocked the blow with her left arm while simultaneously driving the butt of her hand into his nose for a shattering palm-thrust.

The commotion attracted the attention of a nearby bouncer, who appeared in that moment to stop the fight. Vicky quickly explained that she witnessed the whole ordeal and that Selene had merely defended herself after the men got forceful, so the burly employee grabbed the two injured parties by the back of their necks and took them toward the exit. Andreas arrived swiftly thereafter to check on them.

"We're fine," Selene said. "I just need to wash that guy's blood off my hand. I think I broke his nose."

He led them out of the crowd to the ladies' room, where Selene quickly washed her hands and splashed some cold water on her face while Vicky stood by in silence, watching her. As they emerged, they found Andreas still standing outside of the bathroom. When Selene announced they should go home, he escorted them to Vicky's car. The incident had sobered both of them quickly and the cool night breeze refreshed them as they drove with the windows down back to Oia. After driving half of the way in silence, Vicky glanced over at Selene and said, "I can't believe you beat up those two guys. They were so big compared to you. How did you do it?"

"A couple years ago, some overzealous fans got a little too close for comfort so I decided to take a self-defense class," she explained. "I guess that instinct just took over."

"Remind me not to mess with you," Vicky

quipped. "You'd kick my ass."

Chapter Three

As late afternoon on Saturday arrived, Selene paced back and forth in her bedroom, pausing occasionally to stare at herself in the mirror. She had already changed her outfit twice, rejecting both and finally settling on a pair of white mini-shorts and a feminine, low-cut tank top covered with a red, orange and purple geometric pattern that perfectly flowed over her curves. She twisted part of her hair back into a messy bun and let the rest fall down her back, and added large sparkling hoops in her ears. Her hand shook slightly as she applied a bit of mascara and some coral-coloured lipstick. *Why am*

I so nervous?

She didn't have time to figure it out before she heard Nikos knock on the door. Taking a deep breath, Selene grabbed her purse, sunglasses and keys from their place next to the bouquet he had given her, still on display on the kitchen table. Opening the door, she saw he was leaning against the doorway, dressed in a dark pair of jeans, a royal blue dress shirt and a black leather jacket. Her eyes slowly looked up to meet his. *Wow! He's never looked sexier.* His long hair was brushed back and still looked a bit damp and, as he pulled her in to kiss her cheek, she caught a whiff of his cologne, which possessed an evocative and masculine aroma.

"You look amazing," he proclaimed with boyish enthusiasm. "Come, let's go."

Nikos took her hand in his and they walked up the steps, through the crowd on the pedestrian street for a way and then turned down a narrow path that passed between two buildings to the main road, where he had parked his Honda Varadero motorcycle. Nikos hopped on first and started the engine as Selene nervously threw her leg over to sit behind him, wrapping her arms tightly around his waist as they drove down the bumpy, narrow road. The wind was stronger than usual that evening and her hair flapped around her face as Nikos turned the bike to the left at a fork in the road. He followed it down the hillside toward the coast to a sprawling flat area of land below Oia known as Baxedes, a space dominated by farms.

Parking the motorcycle in a gravel lot, Nikos guided Selene across the street to Domaine Sigalas, a family-run winery.

"Have you ever been here before?" Nikos asked.

"No, I haven't."

"It is a very good winery, one of the best on the island. Mr. Sigalas opened it almost twenty years ago. It has been very good for Santorini," he explained. "You will like it."

Despite its reputation, the building itself was not overly large or garish. Its creamy yellow exterior featured rosy stones framing the windows. A wood-slat cover painted slate blue sheltered part of the patio, which wrapped around three sides of the building, creating a gorgeous outdoor space for tastings overlooking the vast vineyard. During a brief tour of the facility, a young dark-haired woman named Maria pointed out that the fields were organized in two sections. Some of the plants sat low to the ground, a traditional pruning technique on the island that she said the locals called "koulara." This basket shape helped protect the grapes from the strong Aegean winds and dry heat, she explained. Others were tied to wooden stakes driven into the ground, allowing the vines to grow vertically up to seven feet tall before the branches curved and fell back to the earth. She informed them that the latter section of vines had the spikes for support as part of an experimental growing technique on the property to help increase their yield. Long drip hoses lined each row in this section about a foot off the ground to provide consistent moisture in the dry climate and, so far, the farm had found success with the new setup.

Maria led the couple to a table in a quiet corner of the patio under a fig tree and next to a short stone wall. Flowers in shades of pink and red grew in pots spaced around the wall, and clippings of the same flowers sat in small vases to decorate each table. The patio itself hosted a scattered selection of black metal tables with faux-marble tops, paired with chairs cushioned with thin back and seat pads covered in natural linen. As they made themselves comfortable, Selene noticed an odd sculpture next to them among the vines that seemed to function as part scarecrow, part art installation. It sort of reminded her of the robot in the movie "Short Circuit."

Handing them each a brochure, Maria informed them they had ten labels available for tastings and asked what kind of wines they liked.

"We like everything," Selene declared, "so you

might as well bring it all."

Nikos laughed at first but when Selene raised her eyes and stared blankly at him, he offered Maria a more manageable request.

"Please start us with your white wines, then we will move on to the reds and finish with the vinsanto."

Maria nodded and disappeared inside, returning promptly with a tray covered in ten petite stemmed glasses, each half filled with at least two-ounce samples of the four white labels and the pale rosé. Selene and Nikos watched intently as Maria opened the two brochures on the table to serve as place mats and set a glass down on top of each wine bottle's image to identify them, describing their characteristics as she worked. After popping back inside, Maria returned once more with a plate of bread drizzled in olive oil paired with various cheeses. She set it down in the middle of their table and told them to enjoy everything.

Raising his sample glass of Assyrtiko-Athiri first, Nikos looked at Selene to make a toast.

"Selene, I am so happy you have come back to the island. I feel very lucky to see you again. To you…" His eyes stared deeply into hers as they clinked their glasses together. As his unflinching gaze continued, she wondered if he really was staring at her so passionately or if she had accidentally read too much into it. The situation made her feel rather strange and curious. In the last five years, nearly all men she had met only wanted a piece of her because of her fame, so this side of Nikos was something for which she was unprepared and it made her feel nervously uncomfortable, giddy and surprisingly lustful all at once. She could hardly believe she was feeling this way about him.

As they sat sipping their wine, he told her of the hard decision he made to leave Athens, a part of him still secretly regretting it, but how he felt compelled to do so for his mother's sake.

"Have you thought of going back?" she asked him.

"I am going back," he replied. "I return a few times a year to visit friends. I try my best to keep in touch. I do not want to lose them too."

His devotion not only to his family but also his other relationships pleased Selene and she liked the honourable man before her. Yet, as he asked her about her music and the recent tour, she couldn't help but wonder what made him interested in her, a young, lonely woman whose life was in ruins. That question rolling around in her mind drove her to knock back her next two wine samples quite hurriedly.

Selene told him more about Roger Carmichael, who had become a force of nature as their manager in the last two years. As the driving arm behind the increasingly commercial tone of their music, he kept pushing her to up her game to sell more records.

"He made me feel as if our previous efforts were inadequate," she told him, as she gulped down the last of the EAN Rosé. "Ryan and Lewis seem content playing Roger's game, but more and more I'm left with a growing sense of dissatisfaction. The new album is selling in spades but, as each tour date passes, I'm growing to hate performing even my own songs.

"By the time we landed in New Zealand to wrap the tour with some local gigs and I received that call about my parents' passing, I felt completely disconnected from the music. I used to love it but now I'm just left with a sense of disillusionment toward the whole industry and my lack of control within it."

As Maria returned to clear their table of empty glasses and provide them with samples of the four red labels, Nikos stared at her as a frown stretched across his brow, and then he took her hand.

"So, what are you going to do about it?" he asked once Maria had left again.

"For the first time in my life," she said frankly, "I honestly don't know."

Stating that fact out loud felt like a knife in the gut for Selene and she continued with her rapid consumption of wine. Nikos watched her intently, and she caught on to the concerned look on his face.

"You're worried about me, aren't you," she suggested.

"Of course," he said. "But you need a night out to let loose."

"And numb my overwrought senses."

"Yes, I see this. You wanted to drink, so I bring you here. At least you don't do this alone. You are with me."

"And you're here to take care of me," she said, flashing him a sassy smile.

"Yes, I am."

"Good," she said before gulping down the rest of the wine in her glass.

Halfway through her samples of red wine, Selene broke her lips away from a glass long enough to speak again.

"You know what the real kick in the ass is with all this?" she asked him, her words slightly slurred. "I let all that mess keep me away from my family. I hadn't even called them in a month and hadn't seen them in nearly a year. Then they died! I was so damn busy working on something I didn't even like doing anymore, and for what? Money, fame, success – none of it means shit!"

She stared blankly into her empty glass and

Nikos sat motionless, saying nothing. *How ironic: I'm getting drunk but am managing to see things more clearly than ever before.* Just then, Maria appeared beside them with their final samples, the two glasses of vinsanto, a sweet dessert wine, famous on the island and made from white grapes but actually possessing a reddish-orange hue.

Selene fingered the stem of her glass in silence as Nikos waited for her to speak again. She felt her next words coming up from a deep, dark place inside her.

"I lost it all, Nikos. My connection to my music, my family; it's all gone now. There's nothing left but fuckin' ashes."

With that, she chugged both portions of vinsanto before he could stop her, and the second of the two glasses shattered on the table as she slammed it back down.

Nikos hurried to pick up the shards and apologized to Maria as she approached. Through her haze, Selene did not notice the sympathetic look Maria gave him but heard her whisper in Greek, "You better take her home now."

Nikos quickly paid their bill and handed Maria a hefty tip for the mess. Then he squatted next to Selene, slung her arm around his neck, lifted her out of the chair and held her upright as she stumbled along with him back across the street to his motorcycle.

"You must hold on tight, Selene," he warned her as they settled in the seat.

"I can do that," she burped as she wrapped her arms around his torso as tightly as she could, the way a child would hug a teddy bear. She nestled her head between his strong shoulder blades and made no attempt to hide the sound of her sniffing his soft hair.

The five-minute drive took more than twice as long during the return trip. Nikos drove extra slowly because of Selene's drunken state. At one point, he had to stop when her grip around his waist loosened and she nearly slid off the bike. He turned his head around and noticed she was falling asleep.

"Selene, you cannot sleep yet," he said as he shook her awake. "You must hold on. We are almost home."

"Okay," she mumbled as she tightened her grip around his waist and they resumed driving once more. "You're coming home with me. That's good. It's lonely there. I don't like lonely."

When he parked in a small empty space close to the steps leading to her house, Selene's clumsy attempt to throw her leg over and get off the bike flopped as she fell to the ground, causing her to roar with laughter. Helping her up from the pavement,

Sunsets in Oia

Nikos said, "You cannot walk now alone."

"I can't walk at all," she laughed at herself and began to hiccup.

"I think it's time for a piggy-back ride," he joked.

"Okay!" she shouted, and with wobbly fervour she leapt onto his back and dug her fingers into him the way a baby koala would ride along with its mother. "Giddy up!"

Selene heard Nikos laugh as he carried her to the cavehouse. Once they arrived at the veranda, she leaned against the wall and watched, her eyes barely open, as Nikos pulled the keys from her purse and unlocked the front door. Feeling dizzy, Selene sensed that she was falling again but Nikos caught her just in time, then carried her barely conscious body inside and put her to bed. The last thing she heard before passing out was his soft voice saying, "You are definitely not a boring date, Selene. Good night, beautiful."

Chapter Four

Early the next morning, a thin layer of high cloud covered part of the sky and a surprisingly strong wind for early summer howled in the air like a woodland wolf or some mysterious creature calling out to an ancient moon goddess. Cars sped by on the street as islanders rushed along the winding mountain road in their morning commutes. The drivers slowed down only at tight corners to avoid oncoming traffic or to pass a caravan of donkeys. The animals, wearing harnesses strewn with tiny bells, were being led to a nearby stairway, winding up the escarpment, by a scrawny man with leathery skin chatting away on his cell phone as he rode the first mule in the line. Then a trio of nearby church bells rang out in song, joining the chorus of morning village noise. It was this sound that caused Selene to sit up abruptly in bed. Her body ached and she couldn't tell which seemed louder: the ringing bells or the pounding in her head. She had only been awake for a few seconds but she could already tell she was experiencing the worst hangover she had had in years. *That's what I get for drinking on an empty stomach.* Her mind was so foggy and discombobulated that it took her a few moments to realize she had spent the night in her parents' bed. She didn't remember crawling into it herself. *Nikos must have put me to sleep here by mistake.*

Feeling a bit strange about having slept in their room, Selene shoved the blanket back from her legs but, feeling a rush of vertigo as she tried to stand, she quickly sat back on the edge of the mattress. As her lungs drew in large, steady breaths, her bloodshot eyes glanced around the room. She affectionately imagined her mother and father there amongst their belongings. A mystery novel still sat on the night stand next to her, a thin layer of dust coating its cover and a piece of red silk protruding from the pages. Next to it rested her mother's old hairbrush, its wooden handle carved from an olive tree. Selene could detect some strands of her mother's hair still tangled around the prongs. Standing now, Selene stumbled over to the tall wardrobe and as she pulled open its two oak doors the sweet scent of her mother's perfume greeted her, preserved on the few clothing items still hanging within. Grabbing the whole lot in her arms, Selene pulled the garments together and buried her face in them, inhaling slowly and deeply. After a minute or so, she pulled away and, with tears in her eyes, focused on one item in particular, the silk bathrobe with its oversized, pastel floral pattern, which her mother always wore while preparing breakfast. Impulsively pulling it off the hanger, Selene slid her arms into the three-quarter-length sleeves and used the pink sash to tie the robe in place.

Next she wandered over to the vanity table and stool facing the adjacent wall, which displayed a decorative mirror in the middle and was surrounded by old photographs hanging in frames. The pictures were mostly more than twenty years old, from the early days of their marriage and when Selene was still an infant. Her eyes settled on one image in particular and she realized it was from the night when her parents first met at the opening party for her mother's gallery. A photographer had snapped it at the perfect moment as the pair stood next to

Sunsets in Oia

a bronze, crescent-shaped sculpture meant to represent Santorini. They were holding flutes of champagne and looking into each other's eyes as if they were the only ones in the room. *That was the exact moment they met.* The photograph showed it truly had been love at first sight. And there, on the corner of the vanity table, sat that same sculpture – Frank had bought it from Cora that night. When she told him it was the most beautiful place she had ever seen, he had imagined himself there on the island with her but did not reveal the fantasy to her until much later.

Selene stepped past the vanity table to her father's dresser in the corner. Most of the drawers remained empty, save for an old sweater, a silk tie and a couple pairs of socks. On top, small personal items cluttered the dresser's surface. In the middle sat an antique metal picture frame divided into three sections and hinged together at the back. The first image was one of Frank as a child with his brother, two sisters and parents back in New Zealand, his homeland; the second was their wedding portrait; and the third was a candid shot Cora had taken of Selene and Frank as he taught her how to ride a bicycle. Selene smiled as she recalled that day more than two decades ago. To the right of the frame sat a small glass box that housed a pair of onyx cufflinks set in gold, a mix of loose coins and a nearly empty box of matches.

The true strength of my father's sentimental nature is embodied in this last item. The thought made her smile as she gently picked it up. Selene had made the lop-sided clay pot, unevenly coated in blue glaze, in art class as a kid. It represented her first attempt at working the wheel during the class' study of pottery and she had struggled greatly to get the clay to cooperate with her small hands. When she had brought the completed project home, ashamed by her results and the low grade it received from the teacher, her dad had looked it over closely and shared a lesson with her that she still remembered: "All great art starts from nothing and there is never a guarantee you'll create a masterpiece. But if you try your best and it comes from the heart, you'll find someone who admires what you create." She felt her eyes water over and could almost hear his rich, calming voice.

At the time, she had expected such an insight-ful quote to come from her mother, who actually worked as a professional artist, but thinking back now, Selene realized it was just the sort of support her father had always given both of them. He had bought her the first guitar she ever owned and stood by her when she decided to study music in university.

And when she had formed the band in her sophomore year, he showed up at every performance and remained their biggest fan. *It all comes back to a crooked old pot.* Turning it in her hands, she noticed it still seemed new, not a single scratch or chip, but the slight rattle that sounded from within surprised her. Looking inside the narrow opening, something shiny caught her eye, so she turned it upside down and shook it a few times until the contents fell out into her free hand.

It was an antique brass key and, after a moment's pause, Selene realized she had seen the key before: it would unlock her father's desk.

Returning the clay pot to the dresser, Selene rushed out of her parents' bedroom and into her own room. Pulling the chair out of the way, she stood before the antique rolltop desk, took a deep breath and found the lock at the base of the cover where it met the flat writing surface. Slowly pushing the fragile key into the hole, she could hear its notches slide against the keyway until it finally aligned in the cylinder. As she turned the key, she heard a loud pop as the lock released the cover. Selene pushed back the desk's tambour to reveal the contents underneath: a collection of pens in a narrow holder, a small notepad, some paperclips and a pair of old reading glasses sitting on top of a leather-bound folder stuffed with papers.

Removing the folder from the desk, she opened it with care and discovered the pages within were her father's poems. *There must be more than thirty of them here, but I've never seen a single one of them.* She recalled their summers together on the island and how her father would rock back and forth in his favourite chair in the main room, reading poetry to them in the evenings as her mother prepared dinner. But the pieces he had read aloud came from the collections on the bookshelf; he never shared any of his own compositions. "They're not ready yet," he told them. He started writing poetry in his twenties and told them he hoped to compile a respectable collection and get them published once he retired.

Selene shuffled along slowly, moving from her bedroom into the front of the house as she stared, wide-eyed, at her father's hand-written pieces. He had written them in the five different languages he knew and used in his work as an interpreter, so Selene could understand only the ones in English or Greek and a bit of the ones in Maori. Flipping through quickly at first, she noticed a date written in the top-right corner of each page, with the oldest pieces at the bottom of the pile. Her hand removed the bottom page from the folder and she noted that its date suggested he wrote the poem a year before her birth.

As she studied the poem's title, a slight bit of movement and a familiar creaking caught her off guard. Her green eyes went wide when she looked to her left – her father's rocking chair was moving back and forth.

It only lasted a couple of seconds before stopping again. *It can't be the wind; the front window is closed tight.* It was an eerie sight, but Selene did not feel scared; in fact, she took the chair's gentle motion as a sign, an invitation of sorts, so she sat down in it to read the one poem, titled "Sunsets in Oia."

> Standing on the lip of this enchanted isle
> Before the dancing sea that swallowed Atlantis,
> Your bare shoulder pressed to mine
> Gives me more warmth than the glowing orb
> Slowly sinking before our eyes.
> And yet, to me, yours shine more brightly,
> Sparkling like the breaking waves below,
> Radiating a shade as rich and precious
> As the earth beneath our toes.
> Under these sunsets in Oia we share
> Together in silence, I watch your beauty
> Evolve with each breathless moment
> Yet I can only stare – helpless, mesmerized –
> In the last of the light that dwindles here.

Then I cling to you as you guide us
Through the dark hours with grace.
Amongst the stars above, you lead me back
To unleash the wild night in me.
Warm in my sleep, I always dream
Of waking to your glow and glory.
You are my rock, my air, my sea.
This place with you is home to me.

As Selene took in those last words, her heart swelled with pride as she sank back into the chair.

"All those years, dad, and I never knew," Selene said aloud, hoping her father could hear her, as she stroked the arm of the rocking chair. "You were always so shy and reserved, shining the spotlight on us instead. But look at this: you're such a talented and passionate writer. I wish you had shared this with me years ago."

Getting to know this side of him thrilled Selene and she indulged in a second reading.

Two hours later, Selene sat silently on her veranda reading from the bunch of papers in the leather-bound folder when Nikos arrived. Dirty dishes lingered in front of her on the table, and she was still wearing last night's clothes, partially concealed by the floral bathrobe.

"What are you reading?" he asked as he

approached, but the sudden sound of his voice startled her. "Apparently, it is very good. You did not hear me coming."

She waved him over to her so he took a seat next to her at the table.

"I found this in my dad's old desk," she said as she cradled the folder. "It's filled with poems he'd written over many years, some even older than me."

"I did not know your father liked to write."

"I had never seen these before today either," she admitted. "He kept them to himself. I think he wanted to publish a whole collection."

Then Selene pulled out the copy of "Sunsets in Oia" and handed it to Nikos. "I want you to read this," she told him. "It's about my mother."

She watched him study the page intently, taking in every word, and he did not look up at her again for several minutes. When he finally finished and handed the piece back to her, they shared a soft smile before she returned it to its place among the others.

"How are you feeling this morning?"

"A bit hung over and quite embarrassed. My memory is fuzzy but I do want to apologize for my behaviour last night. I must have been a horrible date."

"No, not so horrible," he offered reassuringly. "You had a bad night, but I am glad to see you seem much better today. You slept well, yes?"

"I slept hard, but that's not the reason. It was the poems – I've been reading them all morning. I think Dad wanted me to find them."

"Why do you think this?"

"I don't know… It's just a feeling, I guess."

Another moment passed in silence between them as Selene stared down at her father's folder and stroked its cover.

"Come," urged Nikos, "let's go."

"Go where?"

"I have borrowed Pavlo's boat for today. Let's get out on the water. The fresh air will make you feel good, I promise."

Selene hesitated but when Nikos flashed a warm, inviting smile she felt powerless to resist.

"But I haven't even dressed yet. See – I'm still in what I wore yesterday," she revealed as she pulled open her mother's robe.

"Yes, I noticed," he laughed and smiled at her. "You go change, get your bathing suit and I will clean up for you."

He picked up her dishes and tilted his head to the side toward the door to encourage her. Grinning, she stood and followed him back inside and could hear him in the kitchen cleaning the dishes and putting them away as she washed her face and brushed her teeth in the bathroom. In her bedroom, she gently placed her mother's robe on the bed before stripping off her own clothes and tossing them over the back of the desk chair. She pulled a coral-coloured string bikini with wooden beads on its cream-coloured ties from one of her duffel bags and quickly put it on, followed by a pair of denim Bermuda shorts, a white tank top and a thin, crocheted sweater in a rich chocolate colour. Tying her messy hair back into a low ponytail, Selene glanced at herself in the mirror briefly, pulled a beach towel from her other bag and then rejoined Nikos in the main room, where she found him sitting in the rocking chair. It upset her, but she could not figure out why.

"Ah, wonderful! Let's go," he said, standing up quickly.

As they left the cavehouse, Selene glanced back at the moving rocker and it brought a smile to her face as she locked the door. They walked along the village's pedestrian street until they reached the old fort at the northernmost tip of the crescent and then made their way down the stone steps to a small beach and docking area at Amoudi Bay. A few small hotels and cafés were set into the rock nearby and Nikos guided Selene past them to Pavlo's boat. The sight of the old thing inspired Selene to reach into her little purse, pull out a pill case and pop a Gravol into her mouth.

"I know it is old," Nikos said after watching her do this, "but he just finished restoring it and there is a new motor. You are safe."

She nodded and flashed him a smile, her way of thanking him for his reassurance.

A row of vinyl-covered seats lined the rear perimeter, and a large captain's chair was bolted in the middle of the vessel, positioned behind the control panel and fibreglass windshield. Nikos tossed his sandals on deck and helped Selene aboard before untying the lines and pushing the boat back from the beach. Once the water reached the lower part of his thighs, dampening his swim trunks, he threw his leg over the side and pulled himself in. Seated in the captain's chair, he turned the key and the motor roared to life as he turned the wheel to starboard and pointed them out into the bay. As the boat bounced over each oncoming wave and the wind roared by her ears, Selene could not help but flash back almost twenty years to one of the family's first summers on the island when her grandparents had sailed over from Rhodes. The family had climbed aboard her grandfather's smelly fishing boat and, stopping in the middle of the caldera, spent many peaceful hours fishing, swimming and laughing under the hot sun.

Selene didn't acknowledge it when Nikos killed the engine only a few hundred metres from shore. Instead, she sat silently, staring off into the distance with a sad expression on her face.

"What's wrong?" he asked as he dropped anchor and sat next to her.

Shaking her head slightly, she offered a simple explanation: "It's just my head. I'm distracted by my noisy thoughts."

"Ah!" He held up his index finger. "I know the perfect place where you find peace and quiet."

Selene offered him a puzzled frown. "Where?"

Using the same finger, he pointed straight down and then leapt from his seat, pulled up one of the cushions nearby and retrieved two sets of snorkeling gear from within the storage bin beneath the seat.

"What a brilliant idea," she declared as he tossed her one of the bags. Kicking off her flip-flops, she stripped down to her bikini and then slid her little feet into the oversized flippers, securing the straps as much as she could around her bony ankles. Tightening her hair in its elastic, her hands then slipped the mask over her head and positioned it over her eyes and nose. Finally, she adjusted the snorkel tube along the strap so it would comfortably reach her mouth. When she looked up, Nikos stood before her, his gear in place too.

"You look so adorable," he said as he poked the side of her goggles, which made her giggle.

They sealed their lips around the mouthpieces and jumped, holding hands, over the side of the boat. Nikos had anchored Pavlo's boat in an ideal location just off a large piece of volcanic rock jutting out of the sea not too far from the island itself. They were at the far end of this undisturbed and barren piece of earth, which had separated from Santorini centuries earlier during an eruption. Now the rock faced the open waters of the caldera alone. However, the view beneath them revealed that it remained part of the same great curve, the island's roots, which sloped down to the belly of the volcano. As Selene stared through her goggles at the world below her teeming with life, she could see that the landmass dropped off swiftly into the dark depths but the water appeared fresh and remarkably clear, kept clean, she knew, by the strong currents and the minerals released by the submerged volcano. Patches of reef decorated by coral and other plant life caused the rock to sparkle, like crystal, as the sun's rays penetrated the water's surface and kissed the life forms below.

They surfaced to catch a quick breath of air before diving again, continually swimming northeast along the rim. After about fifteen minutes, they reached an area where a peak of rock rose up from the depths but never broke the surface, its face covered in long sea grasses that swayed with the waves. Small dimples and caves were carved into the rock's sides, created over time by the water or burrowing creatures. Surfacing for air once more, Nikos guided her around the rock and pointed out a familiar, man-made shape in the distance, a sunken ship, wrecked on the edge of the reef and covered in a thick film of moss and silt. Small, colourful barnacles had attached themselves to its surface, and a few schools of fish calmly floated around its exterior.

They surfaced for air just then and Nikos pulled his snorkel from his mouth. "I wanted to show you this," he told her.

"Can we go down to it?"

"I have tried before. It is too deep without scuba gear."

"That's okay," she shrugged. "We can just check it out from up here."

They returned the snorkels to their mouths and dove again. After spending a few minutes floating in the area, Nikos guided Selene around the other side of the rock separated from the island, swimming through the more shallow waters between it and the shore, until they reached the boat again. Selene waited as Nikos pulled himself aboard first, then turned back and helped lift her out of the water. They dried themselves and Selene slipped back into her shorts and tank top. They rested for a few minutes as the waves gently rocked the vessel back and forth. Nikos pulled a couple bottles of water from a cooler he had stashed nearby and, after handing one to Selene, he retracted the anchor and readied the boat to head to their next destination.

"Where are you taking me now?" she asked, looking up at him while shielding her eyes with her hand from the intense sun.

"Very special place; you will see."

With that, he turned the key and the motor started once more as he steered them around and pointed them out into the caldera. As they took their time leisurely passing over the deep sapphire waters, Nikos began to hum and sing an old Greek love song. Standing up, Selene walked over and wrapped her arms around him from behind, running her fingers down his chest as she kissed his cheek just below his earlobe.

"My sexy captain…" she whispered to him as he continued to sing.

A little more than a half hour later, he pulled the boat into a tiny docking area at the edge of Nea Kameni, the larger of the two volcano islands rising from the depths in the middle of the submerged caldera.

"Okay, lunchtime," announced Nikos as he tied off the boat.

"And where are we going to do that? You are aware this is an uninhabited volcano?"

"Wherever we want," he said matter-of-factly. "The picnic is in here." Nikos lifted the cooler and tapped its side, and Selene couldn't help but beam.

"Well, you certainly are making up for the date I ruined yesterday, aren't you?"

Nikos only grinned and nodded his head. Reaching for her hand, he helped her from the boat and guided her up the footpath that darted between solidified lava flows, sharp protruding rocks and giant craters. They stopped a couple of times on their way up, where the path wound around to climb the steeply rising hillside, admiring the panoramic views and catching their breath.

It was a hot day but, as they made their way up Nea Kameni's highest rise, Selene grew worried when her feet started to sizzle.

"Ah, Nikos, is it normal that the ground here feels so warm?"

"Yes, it is very hot walking here in summer," he said. "We are very close now to the largest crater and it is still active. The ground gets warmer near it."

"It's active right now?"

"Don't worry," he said. "No lava is there; only a

bit of steam and the smell of sulphur. You are safe with me."

Safe with you on the surface of an active volcano. Still, I have to give the guy points for originality. It's not like I've ever picnicked on the tip of a submerged volcano before.

Nikos found a flat and secluded spot near the path on the highest rise and laid down a blanket for them. As Selene sat down, he began to extract their meal from the cooler: two miniature spinach pies, an eggplant salad, and creamy tzatziki with cucumber and local cherry tomatoes for dipping. The spread delighted her, and he improved it even further when he pulled two tall, chilled bottles of Mythos from the depths of the cooler.

They devoured the meal quickly almost without any conversation, clearly famished after their snorkeling excursion, and then Nikos stretched flat on his back on the blanket to gaze at the bright, clear sky. Selene took this as an invitation and his chiselled stomach made an excellent pillow. He instinctively began running his fingers through her hair and the affectionate but silent communication between them gave Selene a feeling of relaxation and bliss as the earth beneath them warmed their bodies.

"You're not like other guys, Nikos," she said softly. "Why?"

"Most men I meet are interested in me because of the band's success. I always get the sense that they're only curious because they want to hook up with someone famous, and I can't trust them because it's not genuine. But you're different."

"We did not just meet," he pointed out.

"I know. I guess I'm trying to say it feels really nice to just have you here for me."

"I'm glad to be with you, too."

She turned her head to face him and they shared a sweet, soft smile before she closed her eyes as he continued to play with her hair.

Mid-afternoon arrived and Nikos led Selene back down the path and they sailed away from the volcano island toward Santorini.

"One more stop," he called out to her as he turned the vessel southward.

"No complaints here. This is fabulous!"

With a nod, Nikos sped up the boat and they raced over the surface as Selene leaned back in her seat and let the sun's rays kiss her face and neck. About thirty minutes later, she felt the boat slowing again so she opened her eyes to see they were pulling into the bay in front of the island's famous Red Beach, near the coastal farming village of Akrotiri. Selene felt as if they had been transported to another planet and had discovered some lost, aquatic oasis on Mars.

She watched as the waves rushed quickly in and crashed on the shore, where a small strip of beach separated the water from the sheer, crimson cliffs rising hundreds of feet into the air.

"I remember coming here once with my parents when I was a kid," she told him. "The sand felt so hot; we could barely walk on it. I remember asking Mum why the sand looked like a mix of black and red grains. She said it had once been lava rock but the sea had beaten it down and softened it with the constant caress of the waves. I've never seen this place from out on the water though. I forgot how beautiful it is."

The shore appeared fairly quiet that day, with only a few people lingering to soak up the last of the afternoon sun. In the distance, a couple climbed their way up a steep and narrow path that had been made over time by hikers seeking out the secluded and otherworldly beach.

Nikos anchored the boat about twenty-five feet from the rocky edge of the cove below the footpath and ensured the rope felt taut before he called Selene over to the captain's chair.

"You must watch the water does not push us to the rocks. If we drift, turn on the motor and try keeping us in this spot," he instructed her as he started putting his flippers on again.

Puzzled, Selene asked, "Where are you going?"

Securing the goggles over his eyes, he smiled to her and casually said, "To get dinner."

With that, he returned the snorkel tube to his mouth and jumped overboard with a small, netted bag in his hand. Over the next twenty minutes, Selene kept a close eye on the boat's position and watched as Nikos surfaced for air every minute or two before diving down again. In the distance, the sun inched its way down the sky on the other side of the island. *Less than two hours of daylight left.*

Suddenly, she heard Nikos call out from behind her and to the right. As he swam toward the boat, he asked her to remove the beer bottles and food containers from the cooler and fill it with sea water. As he pulled himself aboard again, his dark body shining as the water dripped from his hair and limbs, Selene noticed that his net was no longer empty. Sliding the water-filled cooler to him, she watched as he turned the net inside out to let his catch fall into it. Once the water settled, Selene could not believe her eyes or the luck that her handsome fisherman had. With his bare hands, no less, he had pulled from the rocky ledges near the boat two bulbous sea urchins, a half-dozen meaty shrimp and a small crab.

"We will feast tonight," he proclaimed, his eyes shining.

"I've never prepared live fish like these before," she admitted sheepishly.

"I will teach you," he offered as he placed the lid on the cooler. "We must hurry now though, or we will miss the sunset."

After retrieving the anchor, Nikos started the motor again and nosed the boat around to leave the bay. Crouched on her knees at the stern, Selene watched the cliffs of the Red Beach, now as dark as blood in the evening light, disappear into the distance. The boat bounced over the water and headed north again toward Oia. As they reached the open area of the caldera, the wind died down and the boat easily skimmed over the calm water, now a dark, navy blue. Selene felt a bit chilled as the boat steadily moved along, so she put on her thin sweater. Noticing that Nikos' still-wet body was covered in goose bumps, she grabbed the picnic blanket, shimmied along the seats and then stumbled with the boat's motion until she came up behind him and wrapped them together in it. Its soft, comforting wool and the heat of their bodies warmed each other.

The boat returned them to the waters of Amoudi Bay with about thirty minutes to spare, so Nikos killed the engine and they floated on the open water with an unobstructed view of the setting sun. They sat together in the back bench seats, still wrapped together in the blanket, and Selene rested her head on his shoulder as they watched the sun move lower and lower in the sky. In its last few minutes, its colour deepened to a dark, burnt yellow and the sky around it exploded into a riot of colours – rich oranges and vibrant pinks that, higher up, changed to bright violet and blue – steadily darkening as the sun dipped into the sea and disappeared completely. In that last second, they suddenly heard a spontaneous round of applause begin overhead as the tourists crowding the cliff's sidewalks and verandas showed their appreciation for the natural spectacle. Then the day was over.

"Come," Nikos said softly as he emerged from their shared cocoon. "We should go to your house before it gets too dark."

Selene nodded so Nikos hit the ignition one last time and the boat slowly took them back to the port. As he tied off Pavlo's boat, Selene collected the dishes and bottles from lunch and wrapped them in the blanket to carry them. He grabbed the cooler full of the late afternoon catch and they left the vessel behind, slowly climbing the stairs up to Oia's pedestrian street, which was alive with activity. Weaving their way, hand in hand, through the hordes of visitors seeking a restaurant for dinner or other evening amusements, they finally reached the steps near St. George's Church and Nikos followed Selene as they descended to her cavehouse. Once inside, Nikos carried the cooler to the kitchen and dumped its contents into the sink.

"We will eat the urchins now," he said to her, "then make a soup with the shrimp and put the crab in a pasta."

Selene could feel her mouth water. Walking over to stand next to him, she watched in awe as he pulled the first spiky creature from the sink and flipped it over in his hand to show her its belly. Using the prongs of a fork, he made a circular cut around the base and popped off the shell, revealing the spongy, orange roe inside surrounded by bits of partially digested seaweed stewing in seawater. Nikos tipped his head back and slurped out the liquid and then, using a knife, carved out each piece of roe and put them on a plate.

"Now you try," he said as he handed her the fork and the other urchin. Feeling a bit awkward at first, she tried to copy the steps and, eventually, managed to open the shell and expose the creature's insides.

"Drink the juices," he said encouragingly. Hesitant at first as she looked at it, she finally shrugged and raised the edge to her lips and tossed her head back, letting the salty liquid pour down her throat.

"It tastes like a mouthful of seawater," she said, "but there's a sweet aftertaste."

Angling the knife, she carved out each section of roe with surprising precision and put them on the same plate with the others. After Nikos drizzled the roe with the slightest amount of olive oil and lemon juice, they each snagged a piece in their fingers and began to eat. The slightly slimy texture possessed a sweet flavour that danced on Selene's tongue. "It's delicious!"

Nikos watched, smiling, as she devoured her share of the roe and, once he finished too, they moved on to prepare the shrimp and crab.

As Nikos boiled the shellfish whole in a shallow pot of water with a bit of oil, Selene cleaned and chopped a mixture of potatoes, carrots, celery and peppers for the soup, then prepared some tomatoes, capers, olives and onions to add to the pasta.

Once the shellfish were cooked, Nikos removed the shrimp and crab from the pot and placed them in a bowl of ice water to cool. Using the same slightly oily water for the broth, he added the vegetables to the pot and brought them to a boil, tossing in a few fresh herbs and ground pepper for flavour. While he removed the cooled shellfish from their bowl to chop off the heads and remove the flesh from their shells, Selene started to boil another large pot of water for the pasta, all the while glancing over to watch Nikos work.

There's a graceful efficiency to his cooking skills, which he clearly inherited from his mother.

Poking the vegetables with a fork now to find them nearly tender enough to eat, Selene added the shrimp to the soup, then drained the pasta and combined it with its vegetables, coating the mixture with olive oil, lemon juice and a dash of cream over low heat. Nikos busied himself by setting the table on the veranda and opening a bottle of red wine.

As Selene began to carry the meal outside to join him, she heard her phone ring. Nikos, without saying anything, came back in, took the bowls of food from her and waited while she went to pick up her phone. Selene nearly pressed the button on the touchscreen to answer the call but then noticed the name and number displayed – it was Roger, again. She wrinkled her nose and set the phone down, letting his call go to voicemail. Once they had served, toasted the meal and consumed a few bites, Nikos asked, "Why do you not answer the phone?"

"Ugh," she grunted. "It was Roger. I swear that man is going to drive me mad."

"But why do you not talk to him?" he asked again.

"He just keeps calling me, wanting me to come

home," she explained. "He's pressuring me because I left to take care of the funeral before we finished the tour. We're still under contract for seven more shows around New Zealand and he needs me back."

"Of course he does," Nikos said. "Kauri Spirit does not work without Selene. You are the strongest member, and this Roger knows he can't lose you."

"I know that, Nikos, but it's Roger's insensitivity that upsets me. All he seems to care about is the money, not me. He just doesn't realize that I can't force myself to be ready. But to him, my month-long absence is completely unreasonable."

"Selene, you should take the time you need, but Roger still has a job to do. And so do you. You must be ready by some point."

"I know that, Nikos, I do. It's just that…"

Her voice trailed off as she took a bite of her meal and tried to organize the flurry of thoughts in her head.

"I don't think Roger fully understands what I'm feeling. The way he spoke to me last time, it seemed like he thought I was being dodgy or just pissing around over here," she continued. "It's so much more complicated than he can imagine. I feel as if my old life in New Zealand is trying to come back in, but I'm certain now. I can't go back to it. Not after all this."

Another silent pause lingered over the table as they continued to eat.

"We had a great day today," Nikos said finally. "You seemed like yourself, confident and happy. Now you are sad again…questioning everything. This is not who you are."

Another hush fell over the table as Selene reflected on her changing moods. *Do I really seem that unstable?*

"You cannot go back, Selene," he continued, "even if you want to; life does not work that way. You must find a way to move on as naturally as you can."

"I know you're right; it's just so hard to figure it all out now."

"Roger must know you need to go at your own pace."

"Would you please tell him that? Because he doesn't take it seriously when it comes from me."

They laughed together over this suggestion as they continued with their meal until, a few minutes later, Selene admitted, "You know, I've been trying to do just that – move forward – like you said. That's why I put the house up for sale the other day."

The fork in Nikos' hand crashed down onto his plate.

"Why are you doing this thing?"

"I can't have a house in Greece; I live in

New Zealand."

"But your parents lived in both places. So can you. It's not hard."

"It is too hard!" she argued. "You have no idea how hard it is to be here without them. Everything here is a reminder and it will never be the same. I just can't do it, Nikos. Even this morning, waking in their bed made me feel sick to my stomach."

"No, that was the wine," he pointed out playfully.

She didn't laugh. "I'm being serious, Nikos."

"I am too. This was a home for you with them, and it is still your home. If you sell to someone else, you will not like them living in it and changing it. You will regret it."

He stood to clear the table and, before walking inside, he turned to speak. "You must know what you want, Selene, because after you cannot go back. You don't really want to sell – you know this deep inside. And I don't want you to sell either. You must think hard about what is right."

He turned and disappeared into her house. She wasn't sure if it was the hard decisions she faced ahead or the cool breeze pushing a light mist up to where she sat, but something made her shudder as she sat alone in the dark.

Here I am, alone and stuck between the past and future. I hate this, feeling gloomy and doubting myself all the time. He's right: this isn't me. Damn, do I ever resent this situation. What the hell did I do to deserve going through this alone?

Nikos' voice sounded from inside the cavehouse, asking her to come in out of the cold. The house was in shadows and it took a moment for her eyes to spot him standing next to the counter in the kitchen.

"I have made you a tea with honey and saffron. It will calm you," he offered. "But I must leave you now to get ready for the morning."

"Important plans?"

"I leave tomorrow for Athens to visit friends and do some business."

Her face dropped when she learned he was leaving.

"I will be back in a week," he said as he softly rubbed her bare shoulders, "and I will come see you as soon as I am back. Think about all that I said and, when the time is right, you will know what to do. I will think of you when I am gone."

"I wish you weren't leaving now," she admitted as she looked up into his eyes.

"The time will go fast. But until then…"

His voice trailed off as he moved his head in close to hers and his hands ran down her back until they reached her hips and he pulled her in tightly for a kiss. His soft lips gently caressed hers and his tongue, warm and wet, danced with hers and tasted of olive oil and honey. Giving in to the sudden rush of pleasure, she ran her hands around his neck and into his hair, pulling him in even tighter as their bodies pressed together in the embrace. While one arm stayed tightly wrapped around her lower back, his other hand began to glide up, running along her spine until it cradled the back of her neck in a way that sent a charge, like lightning, all the way down to her toes. She let out a quiet gasp between his passionate kisses as his thumb slid back and, with a light stroke, slowly moved down the edge of her throat until his hand rested on her collarbone. His lips lightened their pressure until she let him pull away. With their noses still touching, one of his hands cupped her cheek as the other slid around and paused on her hip. The look in her eyes begged him to stay.

"I must go," he whispered and briefly kissed her lips once more. Selene stood motionless except for her heaving chest as she struggled to regain control. She stood in silence and watched him walk out her door into the night.

Chapter Five

RING!! RING!!

Selene woke abruptly to the sound of her phone next to her head. As she propped herself up on her elbow in the bed, she flicked on the bedside lamp and glanced at the clock. It read 1:13 in the morning and she groaned as she begrudgingly picked up the phone.

"What? Who is this?" she demanded as she rubbed her eyes.

"Hey, baby. It's Andrew."

Her drowsy mind was suddenly wide awake as the sound of his voice triggered painful memories, forcing a frown to form across her forehead as she recalled the dying moments of their relationship. *This is the last thing I need right now.*

"Why are you calling me in the middle of the night?"

"But it's mid-morning back home."

"That may be so, but I'm not there."

"You're not in Wellington?"

"No, Andrew, I'm not. I'm still in Greece. I had to take care of some things on Santorini. But you still haven't answered my question. Why are you calling? Can't you go bug your new girlfriend? I'm busy sleeping."

"No, I can't. Selene, I left her. She cheated on me."

This little bit of news caused a smirk to spread across Selene's face.

"Ah, karma's a bitch, isn't it?" she jabbed. There was a pause on the line and she decided to use it as an excuse to end the conversation. "Look, Andrew, if that's what you called to say then you've said it. I'm going back to sleep now."

"Wait, Selene, please. That's not all. I wanted to tell you that this whole situation has really made me think. I can't believe I treated you the way I did. I behaved like a jerk and you deserved better – you were right about that. But I realized that I have to make it up to you. You're all I can think about right now. Look, no one else knows about this yet, but I'm planning to retire from football in a couple of months. I want you to use that as a chance to give us another try. I'm not the same man I was before; I know I can be better for you. I won't always be away for matches and I'll be all yours, I promise. I'm serious about this. I still love you, Selene. What do you say?"

"You're kidding me with all this, right?"

"No. I've never been more serious about anything in my life. I heard about what happened to your parents and I'm so sorry I haven't called sooner. But you shouldn't be alone right now and I want to be there for you. I could hop on a plane and join you. We can start fresh."

I had to wake up for this – really?

"No, Andrew. I know you think you're being sincere here but that doesn't change what happened. After the way you betrayed me, I can't just bend to your wishes and give you a second chance – especially not right now with everything that's going on."

"But –"

"It's not going to happen, Andrew. I'm sorry if that disappoints you, but that's the way it is. We're done. We've been done for months. Please, just leave me alone."

She quickly hung up before he could say another

word, set the phone back down on the table and turned off the light. But, even though his offer did not interest her in the slightest, she could not get her mind off the conversation. *Why now?* She stared up through the darkness at the uneven ceiling and struggled for nearly an hour to fall asleep again, regretting even more that Nikos would depart for Athens in the morning.

* * *

Around that same time, Nikos walked into the bathroom of his house to wash the charcoal stains off his cramped hands.

After leaving Selene's cavehouse, he had rushed home to pack for his trip to Athens. Yet, after he finished doing so, he did not go to bed as he should have done. He could not get the memory of their first kiss out of his head, and he suddenly felt an intense urge to draw. Sitting in his old leather chair under the pale glow of the lamp, he propped a giant sketch pad against his bent legs and pulled a fresh piece of charcoal from its box. His hand moved furiously over the page and the hours passed like seconds as he went through sheet after sheet of the bright white paper.

Now, as he left the bathroom and dragged his

tired body through the living room on his way to bed, he glanced over at the leather lounger, draped in a half-dozen new drawings. They were all of Selene. One showed her sitting alone atop her favourite rock, her curly hair flapping in the wind as she stared out at the caldera. Another view had her in the back of Pavlo's boat as she admired the Red Beach in the distance. She lay atop the volcano's rocky bed, wearing her bikini, in a third sketch, while the others depicted portraits of her drawn from different angles.

Cracking his knuckles, Nikos glanced down at his work as a tired but satisfied smile spread across his face. Then he flicked off the lamp and stumbled into bed, where he quickly fell asleep.

Chapter Six

Two mornings later, Selene woke yet again to the sound of her phone ringing next to her on the nightstand. She rolled over and groggily answered it, greeted by the excited sound of Vicky's voice.

"Good morning, Selene. I have wonderful news for you. I have a lovely couple from France here at the office. They have been traveling on the island this month and love it here. When they learned you are selling your house, they said they want to view it right away. Can you tidy up and have it ready for them to visit this afternoon?"

Selene could hardly digest this bit of news.

After a few seconds of silence, Vicky asked, "Selene, are you there, dear?"

Selene cleared her throat. "Uh, I think so." *I can't believe I'm agreeing to this.* "Tell them you'll bring them by around two o'clock."

"Wonderful, dear!" Vicky exclaimed loudly in her ear. "I have a good feeling about this. See you later today."

Selene heard a click in her ear but she lay frozen, her phone still pressed to her face. *Am I really ready for this?* There was not much choice in the matter, she realized, for she had just agreed to the thing. She pushed back the sheet covering her, swung her legs over the edge and begrudgingly got out of bed. Either way, now she had work to do. A gurgle sounded from within as she stood. She decided to have breakfast first before setting about to clean and prepare the house for the potential buyers.

The cavehouse felt stuffy and humid that morning, so she walked to the front wall and pushed the window wide open before returning to the kitchen. Pulling food from the refrigerator, she prepared a breakfast of fried eggs and grilled tomatoes seasoned with pepper and rosemary, adding a thick slice of crusty bread drenched in honey. Pleased with the plate, she carried it and a large glass of juice out to the veranda to enjoy the meal and breathe in some much-needed fresh air. Slowly picking away at the meal, Selene was distracted by the day that had been forced upon her with the visit of the French customers. *What did you think would happen when you put the house on the market?* Even with a suffering economy, she knew that property on Santorini – and especially a traditional cavehouse in Oia – would always attract foreign investors hoping to take advantage of troubled times that drove down market prices.

Nearly an hour later, Selene carried the dishes inside and took a long, hot shower, hoping to clear her head. By the time she finished and turned off the water, she felt renewed and calm. Wrapping the towel around her body, she walked back to her bedroom, dressed herself in an old t-shirt and shorts, and pulled her hair back and tied it into a high bun. Hanging the damp towel in the bathroom, she headed into the kitchen intending to pull some cleaning products out from under the sink.

The first creak was soft but each one after grew louder. Selene slowly turned around to look. Her gaze fell upon her father's old chair as it rocked back and forth at a steady pace, appearing to move under its own power. Her body froze in place as she stared, struggling to process what her eyes were seeing, and her mouth parted slightly as she exhaled a bursting gasp of disbelief. *It's doing it again. I'm going mad. This can't be real.*

She remembered the open window and turned to close it, assuming the rocking would stop. As she took her first step, the creaking sound ceased. She whipped her head around to see the chair motionless once more. *What's causing this?* For a minute she let herself think that, just maybe, it could be her father's ghost sending her a sign. She shook her head, knowing it was a silly thought, but she allowed herself to wonder what it could mean, what he was trying to say to her. *Dad, is that you? You'll have to speak louder than that.*

She walked over to the rocker and knelt in front of it, as if before some sort of altar.

"Dad, if you can hear me and it's really you moving your chair, I don't know what to make of it," she said softly as she stared at it, assuming his spirit might be sitting there in front of her. "You made it move the first time when I pulled that poem from your folder and I thought it meant you wanted me to read it. Now you choose today to do this again… Why? You have to tell me what this means. I don't know what to do."

She bowed her head and allowed a single tear to fall from her eyes to the floor as she briefly closed her eyelids.

After a quick pause though, Selene shook her head. *If I continue thinking this way, I really will go crazy.* She went on as before and pulled the basket of cream cleanser, glass cleaner, scrub brushes and rags from under the sink and went about her work, moving from room to room, leaving no spot untouched until, two hours later, the house appeared spotless and sparkling and ready to receive the potential buyers. Finished and satisfied with how nice things smelled now, she grabbed her sunglasses and guitar case from her room, locked the door behind her and headed down to the flat rock that jutted out from the cliffside. She let her legs dangle over the edge as she sat down, pulled the instrument from its case and decided to play to the wind.

She let her hair down so it could flap about in the breeze as she began to strum. At first, the series of chords sounded random and blended together to represent her melancholy state, but something changed. As the warm sun beat down on the back of her neck and the salty air refreshed her lungs, she soon felt her spirit lightened as the guitar's vibrations pulsed through her body and memories of previous summers on the island filled her with thoughts of happier times. She put the pick back in the case and began to pluck the strings the way her uncle, Alex, showed her years ago while teaching her some traditional Greek songs. He had brought his wife and two young daughters down from Thessaloniki so the two families could visit with each other. Selene smiled to herself as she rehearsed some of the old tunes they had played together all those years ago while her mother sang along and the others danced together on the veranda. Something about those songs filled Selene with a sense of peace. The intricate combination of sounds and repetitive melodies, along with the fresh breeze whirling around her, soothed her spirit. Her mind drifted back to the family's visit to Red Beach all those years ago, when her mother talked of the waves softening the sand, and it made her smile. *This music is doing the same thing for me.*

Hours later, when the sun hung high in the sky and her watch told her she had to head back, Selene returned the guitar to its case and slowly climbed the steps to the house. Less than fifteen minutes later, Vicky arrived with the French couple and Selene welcomed them inside.

"Olivier and Hélène, I'd like you to meet the owner, Selene Doherty," Vicky said in a highly professional tone.

"Bonjour, and welcome to Oia," Selene greeted them and shook their hands.

Olivier looked to be in his mid-forties and had

bright, piercing blue eyes, a slightly crooked nose and salt-and-pepper hair trimmed to a length of about an inch long on top tapering to nearly a buzz around his ears and the back of his neck. He dressed handsomely in designer jeans and a grey cashmere sweater with expensive Italian leather shoes. Hélène was the perfect arm candy: about fifteen years his junior, she had silky, auburn hair, tanned skin, large breasts and wore a tight-fitted summer dress with plenty of expensive gold jewellery.

As Vicky walked them around the cavehouse, telling them about its history and features, Selene watched the couple and the vibes she sensed from them concerned her. Once the tour had finished, the clients paced around again while softly speaking to each other. Selene managed to discern, with the bit of French her father had taught her, that they were discussing a total renovation of the house, gutting the place and remaking it completely in their own image. Selene suddenly felt nauseated, so she politely dismissed herself and retreated to the veranda.

They stayed for nearly an hour. As they left, Vicky told Selene the couple planned to view a few more properties that week but they were considering her place and would have Vicky get in touch with her if they decided to make an offer. Selene closed the door, leaned against it and, with a heavy feeling in her chest, looked around at her house, imagining what it would be like to say goodbye to it forever. As her eyes settled on her father's rocking chair, it began to move again.

Chapter Seven

By late Friday morning, Selene had been on the island for two and a half weeks. It was unseasonably hot for mid-June and the town bustled with activity because three cruise ships had anchored in the caldera a few hours earlier. The tourists were flooding the village's tiny streets, enjoying brunch at nearby restaurants and shopping for mementos.

Selene sat in her father's rocking chair sipping a cup of tea as she read his poems over and over. A knock on the door jolted her from her reverie. *Nikos is back early!* She jumped to her feet, set the folder on the kitchen table and opened the door to greet him with a kiss.

"Ryan?"

Selene became best friends with Ryan Stewart after meeting him on their first day of class at university back in Wellington. He had moved to the city from the South Island to attend school and did not know many people there at that point, so they quickly became inseparable. Ryan had suggested that they form a band the following year and, by being on the road together over the years for tours, he had come to learn all of her moods – good and bad – and could now recognize when she needed help even without asking for it.

Selene stared, wide-eyed, jaw dropped, not even sure it was him initially. He had shaved off his beard, and his shaggy brown hair now looked short and layered with a sweep over his forehead to one side, tapering to a buzz over his ears.

"Oh my god, Ryan!" she exclaimed as she gave him a quick hug. "You look so different. It's been years since I've seen you with hair this short."

"Yeah, well, Nana always hated it long so I cut it all off two weeks ago just before I went to visit her," he said as Selene welcomed him inside. She led him over and he sat down beside her on the loveseat.

"So you've been in London?"

"Until yesterday. After the funeral, I stuck around

in Athens for a while, just in case you needed me. Plus I'd never seen that city without being there for a gig, but when you skipped town to come here, I decided to go visit Nana, Uncle John and my cousins in England."

"That's lovely. How are they?"

"They're all well. Nana's health has improved a lot since she was discharged from the hospital so it felt good to see her in her usual high spirits," he said and then paused. "They all asked after you. They're worried. After a couple weeks without hearing from you, I started worrying too. Then Roger called me."

"Oh god – what did he tell you?"

"He said you two got into it on the phone. Said you sounded really mad at him for mentioning the leftover shows and that you've been ignoring him ever since."

"Damn right I ignored him. He had no right to pressure me like that."

"But it's his job, Selene," he begged. "He told me he's never heard you sound that way, like you weren't yourself at all. And you know Roger: he's all business. So for him to be so worried about your wellbeing, I figured it had to be really bad, so I hopped on a plane to check on you."

"I appreciate the sentiment, Ryan, but I'm doing fine," she said, her eyes cast downward as she fidgeted with the drawstring on her shorts.

"No, you're not, Selene. I can tell," he said and shot her the look he always had to call her bluff. "You look exhausted."

"Oh, thanks. That makes me feel so much better," she blurted out as she stood and began to pace around the room to feel less cornered.

"I'm serious, Selene." He stood, walked over to her and stopped her pacing by resting his hands on her shoulders, giving her a moment to calm down. "So if it makes no difference to you, I'm just going to hang out here for a few days to see if I can't coax out that wild, fun and crazy Selene that you're hiding."

She could tell he would not budge on the subject; he was even more stubborn than her, so she decided to indulge him.

"Fine, stay as long as you'd like. I'm stuck here until the house sells anyway. You must be starving," she said. "I'll make you some brunch."

"Thanks, mate."

Selene set about cooking some eggs – scrambled, of course, the only way he would ever eat them – and also served him a bowl of Greek yogurt with honey and berries. They sat on the veranda, sipping tea together. She realized, as she watched him eat, how glad she felt to have his company. Things had been very quiet for her the last few days. Vicky had

Sunsets in Oia

not brought anyone new to view the house and, with Nikos out of town, she felt lonely. She and Ryan didn't talk much at first though, and she noticed he seemed tired, so she suggested he take a nap.

"I could use one, actually," he admitted. "I had an overnight flight from Heathrow so I didn't sleep much."

Of course he didn't. He's never been good at sleeping on airplanes.

"I'll put some fresh sheets on the bed in my parents' room and you can rest in there," she said as she collected his dirty dishes from the table and carried them back into the kitchen. He followed her inside and helped her strip the bed.

"Okay," she said as they finished making the bed, "sleep as long as you'd like. I'm going to go outside so you can rest in quiet."

He nodded sleepily to her and she left the room, grabbed her guitar case, and walked out of the house.

Two and a half hours later, Ryan emerged from the cavehouse, freshly showered and alert, and the sun hit him with a blast of hot air like one would feel upon opening an oven. A sudden burst of salty wind rose up from the sea to greet him, and it carried with it the faint sound of Selene's guitar and her soft yet powerful voice. He followed her sound, making his way down the escarpment, until he finally spotted her in the distance, sitting on the edge of a flat piece of rock that jutted out from the cliffside. She was singing "Hold On," an old song by Sarah McLachlan, her favourite artist. The bitter-sweet tune rang out and each note seemed to linger in the air over the caldera, and even though there was obvious melancholy in Selene's voice, she had never sounded more earnest and beautiful.

As her pick plucked the song's final note, Selene realized she wasn't alone when she heard a single pair of hands applauding from behind her. Whipping her head around, she looked up and saw Ryan standing on the steps about fifteen feet above her. He continued to clap for her as he made his way down the last steps and hopped over onto her rock.

"Stop that," she said with a laugh. "You're being silly." But then she saw the look on his face and sensed his sincerity.

"And to think I was so worried about you! You've never sounded better."

He sat down beside her and flashed a warm smile her way, then drew in a deep breath and said, "You've got quite the view here." Gulls hovered in the air, floating on thermals. Selene pointed out the catamarans and old schooners packed with tourists as they slowly moved with the wind over the water of the caldera, which appeared fairly calm that afternoon and glittered as each small wave caught the sun's light. In the distance, a large ferry moved southward. "That one's probably heading to Crete," she said. Below them to the right, they noticed a group on a small pleasure-craft jumping overboard for a scuba dive. She heard Ryan gasp as he continued to look out, barely blinking to take it all in.

"Hearing all those stories from you about this place, I can see now why you love it here so much."

"Yeah, I did."

"Past tense?"

"It just doesn't feel the same anymore, you know?"

He nodded, sighed, and turned his head to face her.

"Is that why you're selling the house and just had me sleep in the master bedroom instead of the other one?"

Selene looked down into her lap, awkwardly shifted her weight where she sat, and then whispered softly, "Yes."

"Do you honestly think that avoiding their room and getting rid of the house they left to you will make you feel better?"

"No." Her barely audible voice sounded shaky and her shoulders fell forward into an uncomfortable hunch.

"I don't get it, Selene. If you don't think that what

you're doing will help you move on, then why do these things at all?"

"Because it's the only move I know how to make right now." The words burst out of her and, as she looked at him, giant tears fell from her eyes. Her back curled and, while still cradling the guitar, she buried her face in Ryan's shoulder as he stroked her back.

With a light squeeze to her shoulder that raised her gaze to him again, Ryan smiled and said, "I think, secretly, you wanted to come back here. You could have easily hired someone to show and sell the house without you being on the island, but you flew in anyway. I know it must feel strange now being here without your family, but I think you should give this place another chance. Who knows – you just might learn to love it all over again as your own. Think of how great it would be to come here, escape the wet New Zealand winters and have this as your own home away from home. You've never been good with the cold weather."

Selene's brow furrowed and she chewed her bottom lip. *It's not a bad idea, but I don't know. I can't even think about that right now.*

"You don't have to decide this second," he offered, "but just promise me you'll think about it, think about what would make you happy for the long term." When she nodded and managed a small smile, he added, "Now, in the meantime, I think you need to show me around this gorgeous town of yours. We should have some fun while I'm here."

"What do you want to do?" she finally asked.

"Well," he said as he rubbed his hands together, "first I think I should lie out on your patio and get some sun on these pasty legs of mine."

This made both of them laugh until Selene managed to say, "Okay, then what?"

"Then I am going to take you out for dinner at your favourite restaurant in town – my treat," he declared. "And then we should go out and party. Does this place have any clubs?"

"Yes, one. It's called Hasapiko."

"Hasapiko," he repeated slowly to get the pronunciation correct. "Good – we'll go there and you can show me a good time and we'll party with the locals."

Oh no. He's probably going to get drunk on Ouzo and I'll be stuck nursing his hangover in the morning. Still, she felt strangely excited about showing him around Oia.

The two friends went inside and changed into their swimwear, and Selene pulled the cushions off of the patio furniture to create a soft surface on the floor of her veranda, which she covered with beach towels, while Ryan applied a generous amount of sunscreen to his exposed skin. They lay down next to each other, closed their eyes and let the heat of the Mediterranean sun soothe them into a languorous state, only moving enough to flip over to keep their skin exposure even. At one point, around four o'clock, they got up and disappeared inside to drink large glasses of Greek frappé, sweetened with brown sugar. They also scarfed down a turkey sandwich dressed with olive paste, Swiss cheese and tomatoes on a fresh baguette, which they split between them. Then they returned to lounge on the veranda again.

A little before seven o'clock as the sun dipped low in the sky and the veranda's sparkling surface faded under the growing cover of the cavehouse's shadow, the pair finally rose from their comfortable tanning bed. Selene's skin glowed with a deep bronze shade that made her look like an ancient goddess immortalized in an artist's statue, while Ryan's pale Celtic skin had turned pink from hours of exposure and displayed several new freckles on his face, arms and chest.

"That might hurt in the morning," Selene said to him with a slight snicker.

"Nah, I'll be fine," he replied as he examined himself. "Hope I don't peel though. But look at you – you're as brown as a bean! How'd you get so dark?"

"It helps to have Greek and Maori blood in me,"

she bragged. "I've never had a burn in my life."

As he helped her retie the cushions to the patio chairs, he looked up at her and asked, "Do I really look that red?"

"A bit," she admitted, "but I have just the thing. It's a cream infused with aloe and olive oil. It'll help keep your skin moist and by the morning that burn will be a nice, light brown."

"Really?" he asked as they walked inside, questioning the powers of the moisturizer.

"I promise," she assured him. "I should have known this Mediterranean sun would be too much for you, even with sunscreen."

She went into her bedroom, pulled the bottle out of her duffel bag and tossed it to him. Once he had left the room she dressed herself in a shin-length maxi dress made of white linen and a lavender-coloured wrap sweater of knitted cotton, which she twisted into a design just below her bust and secured the ends in a knot behind her back. Her fingers slid the hooks of a pair of long chain earrings, decorated with emerald-coloured Swarovski crystals, into her ears. She left her long curls down to fall along her neck to the middle of her back. After putting on a pair of white sandals, she met Ryan at the front of the house. He had changed into a pair of skin-tight black jeans, his favourite Led Zeppelin tour t-shirt, partially covered by a zippered hoodie, and a pair of red Converse high-tops.

"So, where am I taking you to dinner?" he inquired as she locked the door.

"To my favourite place, just as you said," she hinted. "It's called Terpsi. It's just up the street a little way."

Selene guided Ryan up the winding steps to the pedestrian street, where they turned left into the crowd of tourists and slowly moved through the people until they reached the restaurant. The exterior of the building, painted in a weathered coral shade, did not appear overly impressive or inviting compared to the neighbouring buildings, but as soon as they stepped inside it was easy to see why Selene favoured the place. Terpsi, which the owner marketed as a music café, had Euro-lounge and instrumental folk music softly playing from small, wall-mounted speakers in nearly every corner of the two-storeyed dining space. A handsome, slightly chubby man, with a thin goatee and bright hazel eyes, greeted them at the entrance, asking where they would like to sit. Selene told him they would like to go upstairs, so he directed them past the large bar along the left of the front hall, impressively stocked with dozens and dozens of different liquors from all over the world. The host pointed up the

Sunsets in Oia

stairs at the back and told them, in broken English, to enjoy their meal.

Ryan and Selene climbed the single flight of winding cement steps to the upper level and selected a table near the middle of the dining area. The room, left open to the breeze, had an impressive panoramic view of the caldera with shade provided by strips of woven canvas similar to those at Pavlo's restaurant. The tables, elegantly but simply dressed with white linen tablecloths, featured red runners on which rested a single potted cactus. Only three other tables were in use upstairs; Selene suggested the evening winds had discouraged the rest of the customers, who chose a more sheltered dining area downstairs. "I hope you don't mind the breeze."

As they sat down at their table, Selene and Ryan were greeted by their waiter, who introduced himself as Roman. Selene noticed he was dressed in a dark pair of jeans, with the restaurant's uniform red golf shirt and a thin, black sweater. He was tall with broad shoulders, sandy hair, a tiny mouth with pale lips, small but bright eyes and a long, straight nose framed by prominent cheekbones. Selene could tell by his accent that he came from somewhere in northeastern Europe, but he managed to greet them in perfect Greek before switching to English for Ryan. Presenting them with menus, Roman proceeded to recite the evening's specials and then asked for their drink order. Selene knew Ryan still did not appreciate wine very much, so she ordered a bottle of Mythos for each of them. Roman returned so promptly with their drinks that they barely had time to glance at the menu. Selene watched as Roman stepped away to give them more time and glided between the other occupied tables to check on his patrons. When she next glanced up, he stood waiting in his corner by the top of the steps, stoic and postured with his chest proudly pushed out, so Selene signaled for him to return to their table to take their order.

Within the first few bites, Ryan declared the meal exquisite, devouring his lamb paired with risotto and vegetables while Selene savoured her generous serving of moussaka and salad.

"I can't remember the last time I had food this good," Ryan exclaimed as he swallowed the last bite of his dinner and caressed his bloated stomach. "Is it like this everywhere here?"

"Pretty much," she told him with a smile. "Welcome to Greece, mate."

All around them, the sky had transformed into stunning shades of rose, blood-orange and violet as the sun set behind them. The chilly wind was picking up a bit, so Ryan asked Roman to bring

Sunsets in Oia

each of them a double espresso and they chased their meals with the scorching and strong coffee while they watched the world around them quickly go dark. As they readied to leave, Selene and Ryan observed the entire island now lost to the blackness, save for the specks of light illuminating the cliffside towns dispersed around the crescent. As promised, Ryan picked up the cheque and left Roman a generous tip, for which he dipped his head and bent slightly at the waist to each of them. On their way out the main door, the goateed host offered them a similar bow and thanked them for their business. Selene and Ryan slowly made their way down the pedestrian street to walk off their dinners before they headed to Hasapiko.

It was nearly ten o'clock before they arrived at the club, already half full with a mixture of young tourist couples and groups of locals. The smell of cigarette smoke filled the air in the tiny club, which consisted of just two connected rooms. The long bar stretched across the corner of the first room and a DJ station occupied another corner in the second room, with stacks of CDs filling a shelving area on the wall behind the DJ. Dance and hip-hop songs from the '90s blasted from the speakers. They selected a table in the front corner of the second room. A woman with long, frizzy curls, who looked as if she would blend in well with a group of gypsies, brought them small bowls of thinly cut carrot sticks and mixed nuts. She returned a few minutes later with their beers, and they sat there, sipping away, as a few of the other guests danced in the limited area of open floor space.

Within an hour, as usual, Ryan had managed to befriend half a dozen people seated nearby and, pushing the tables together, the large group indulged in a bottle of Ouzo that Ryan ordered. It was the same story as almost any other night when they had gone out drinking together: Ryan inevitably became the life of the party and brought together people who were otherwise strangers in order to create a scene of unpredictable, frenzied merriment and over-indulgence. As she watched her best friend pound back shot after shot of Ouzo, Selene cursed herself, but she felt delighted to see him enjoying the evening and eventually she gave in to the fun. At one point, an Australian couple recognized them as members of Kauri Spirit and worked their way into the group, insisting on buying another bottle of booze for the table so they could do shots with their new celebrity friends. Selene tried to downplay their status but the others soon whipped out cameras to have their pictures taken with the musicians. By the end of the night, the two of them had turned the

Sunsets in Oia

whole bar into their entourage, celebrating with the strangers and staff until four in the morning when they finally stumbled back to Selene's cavehouse.

Chapter Eight

At midday on Monday, Nikos rushed down the steps to Selene's cavehouse with a happy swagger. He had spent a wonderful week in and around Athens, reconnecting with friends over dinners on the town and during a camping trip. He was now returning to Santorini with a renewed sense of worth too, having collected the commissions on several pieces of his art that had recently sold in the city. Yet, with each day of his absence, he thought constantly of Selene. The time had passed quickly but he loathed being parted from her, and now he raced toward her home, hoping to fulfill the fantasy growing in his mind all week. He longed to kiss her again and thought of nothing else but scooping her into his strong arms and carrying her to bed.

By the time he reached her front door, his heart pounded in his chest with excitement and anticipation, and just the feeling of the smooth wood against his knuckles as he knocked managed to arouse him. He felt like a teenaged boy again, dizzy from the stimulating surge of testosterone rushing through his veins.

* * *

The sound of a hand rapping against Selene's front door triggered a stir in the house as she shouted, "Can you get that?" Within seconds, a handsome young man with brown hair and a light tan pulled the door open, waiting shirtless and curious in the entrance. The man's buff, half-naked body triggered an uncontrollable jealous twinge that caused a scowl to form on Nikos' face.

"Can I help you, mate?" Ryan asked politely, but Nikos remained silent and frozen as he stared back at him in contempt.

When Selene emerged from the bathroom, her hair still wet from a shower and her body wrapped in a towel, she glanced over to see the two men in her doorway.

"Nikos!" Her voice's pitch sounded high with exhilaration when she spotted him and ran to greet him at the door. Holding the towel in place with one hand, she pushed up onto her toes, threw her free arm around his neck and planted a quick, wet kiss on his pursed lips. As she pulled away, his eyes settled coldly once more on her mystery guest, who stepped to the side as Selene grabbed Nikos' hand and brought him inside.

"I'm so glad you're back," she said gleefully and then, noticing Nikos was watching Ryan like a hawk, shook her head as her manners returned to her. "I'm so sorry – Nikos, this is my best friend and drummer, Ryan Stewart. Ryan, this is Nikos Kafieris. We've known each other since we were kids."

Nikos' gaze softened and his brow shot up as he recognized the man's name. "I apologize," he said sincerely with a hint of embarrassment. "You look very different from the pictures in the CD."

"Oh, yeah," Ryan agreed as he shook Nikos' hand. "I just got my hair all cut off. Selene barely recognized me at first."

"Ryan popped in a few days ago to check up on me," Selene explained. "He's been keeping me company while you were in the city."

"I see," said Nikos as he nodded slowly. "It is nice

Sunsets in Oia

to finally meet Selene's best friend."

"You too, Nikos," Ryan replied. "She's told me quite a bit about you since I arrived. We were just heading down to the beach if you'd like to join us."

Nikos nodded and Selene disappeared into her bedroom to slip into her bathing suit. Emerging moments later wearing a sheer bronze cover-up over a black-and-white tankini, with white flip-flops on her feet, she tossed each man a towel and the threesome hiked down the steps until they reached a rough, rocky path that took them the rest of the way to the shoreline, where a narrow patch of sand nestled against the escarpment. They were the only ones there at the secluded spot, and having a private place at the water's edge made for a care-free and enjoyable afternoon. With their towels grouped together on the sand, Nikos removed his t-shirt while the other two relaxed in their swim-wear as they all made themselves comfortable on the soft ground. With the scorching sun high in the sky, Nikos entertained them with tales of his trip to Athens as they lay on the sand. After an hour, Selene felt hot and perspiration had started beading on her skin so she suggested they go for a dip in the cool water.

"But I am in my clothes," Nikos stated.

"Then swim in your boxers, mate," Ryan suggested

as he sat up.

Nikos rose to his feet and, staring straight into Selene's eyes, slowly undid the button and zipper of his shorts, letting them drop to the ground to reveal a pair of fitted, navy boxer-briefs with red trim. A lustful gaze passed between them as Selene stood and led Nikos by the hand into the low waves.

Selene, Nikos and Ryan played in the water for a couple of hours that afternoon, splashing about as if they were children. Later that day, Nikos parted from them briefly to go home and put on clean, dry clothes before meeting with them once more to treat them to dinner at Argonaut.

That evening, Selene greeted Nikos when he arrived at the cavehouse. She and Ryan followed him as he led them into the heart of the village. While deep in conversation as they walked along the pedestrian street, a boy in his early teens, wearing tattered jeans and a grubby t-shirt, burst through the crowd at top speed and smashed into Selene and Ryan as he ran through their line. As this happened, a clamour erupted in the crowd ahead of them as a woman's shrill voice screamed, "Thief! My purse! Stop him!"

Nikos' head whipped around and he spotted the boy running away, the woman's purse firmly tucked under his arm. Selene watched as Nikos bolted after him and managed to close the gap between them quickly, the thief's path obstructed by the crowd heading to the tip of the island to watch the sunset. Selene and Ryan chased after Nikos and watched, shocked, as he took hold of the fleeing thief by the shoulder. The boy spun around, his free arm swinging wildly at Nikos to defend himself, but Nikos deflected the blow and delivered a swift jab to the kid's gut, which caused him to drop the purse. Nikos retrieved the bag as the boy cursed at him in another language and gripped his sore belly while darting into the crowd again.

"Aren't you going to go after him?" Ryan asked as he and Selene reached Nikos.

"No. I am not police," he shrugged. "I just want to stop him from getting this. He's probably the kid of a foreign worker. He will be sore tomorrow and learn his lesson."

"I can't believe you just chased after him like that," Selene gushed. "He was going so fast and could have pulled a knife on you. That was really brave."

Nikos smiled at her compliment just as a tiny Asian woman in a tight dress and stilettos uneasily jogged toward them.

"That's my purse," she cried as she saw it in Nikos' hands. "Thank you for stopping him."

"Is it really yours?"

"Yes. You can check my ID inside," she offered.

Nikos popped open the magnetic metal lock at the top of the little clutch and pulled out the ID card, which the owner had tossed in loosely among a collection of euros, credit cards, makeup and condoms. He glanced at the photograph on the Singaporean driver's licence and then back at the young woman.

"You have travelled far," he said as he placed the ID back in the bag and returned it to her. "I hope this does not ruin your trip."

"Oh, no. You just saved it. Thank you so much, sir. How can I repay you?"

"No need. Please enjoy yourself and hold on to that thing," he said with a smile.

The young woman nodded, bowed to Nikos, thanked him again and then turned away.

"I can't believe that just happened," said Selene.

"I know," Ryan added. "Does that happen a lot here? Should I be guarding my wallet?"

"No. You are very safe here," Nikos stated. "The island is peaceful."

"He's right. I've spent countless summers here and have never witnessed something like that," Selene added.

"It's the economy," Nikos suggested. "It makes some people desperate. But we forget this now and enjoy dinner."

Selene could not get the image of Nikos running after the young bandit out of her head as she continued to glance up at him while they walked the rest of the way to Argonaut. She realized the incident and Nikos' heroic action had managed to turn her on.

The restaurant, a small grill house in the middle of the village, featured seating on its colourful outdoor patio. Bowed metal rods hovered over the space and held up dark fabric netting for shade. The exterior walls warmed the space in their shades of sunset orange and brick red, while two rows of broad wooden tables were surrounded by old oak wine barrels that had been converted into chairs with multi-coloured cushions where the lid had been. Known for its expertise at preparing meat and fish as well as strong drinks, Argonaut had turned into a favourite hangout for locals and curious tourists due to the fact that it hosted live Greek music every night.

Over the next three hours, the trio feasted on souvlaki, salmon and veal plates with roasted potatoes and consumed copious amounts of wine and beer while listening to the musicians perform. The evening culminated when Nikos encouraged them and other patrons to join him in a traditional Greek line dance. They wrapped their arms around each other's shoulders as Nikos led the group up and down the central aisle and out into the street and neighbouring parking lot while the band played on and on for them. Nikos took the opportunity to show off a bit too, releasing himself from Selene briefly to spin around or kick his leg into the air, which triggered cries of "Opa!" from the others. He appeared light on his feet and his energy seemed infectious – the performance could put even Anthony Quinn's "Zorba" act to shame. Ryan kept eyeing Nikos, which Selene noted, assuming he felt jealous of the handsome Greek man who had stolen the spotlight. But the glowing smile on Selene's face quickly sated his ego as she danced between them, laughing with each step.

Walking home together, Selene kept her arms linked with each man as they strolled along the stone pedestrian way but, as they reached the steps down to her cavehouse, Nikos halted.

"I will go home now," he said softly.

Selene looked up at him with big, sad eyes and her lips turned down slightly in disappointment.

"Nikos, it was a pleasure," Ryan said as the two men shook hands. "I know I've sort of stolen Selene's time from you, but I'm heading back to Wellington in a day or so. I can see I'll be leaving her in good hands. Thank you for dinner tonight. It was grand to meet you, mate."

"Thank you," Nikos responded graciously. "I am glad to meet you." He turned back to Selene and squeezed her hands tightly as he said, "Have fun with Ryan and I will see you once he has gone."

Her head nodded and Nikos kissed the back of her hand before leaving, she assumed, to spend the night alone in his own bed.

* * *

In mid-morning on Wednesday, Selene stood in the doorway of her parents' bedroom as she watched Ryan hastily shove the last of his belongings back into his suitcase. His flight was leaving in just over an hour and a taxi would arrive at any moment along the main road to take him to the airport.

"Look, Selene," he started, as his fingers pulled the zipper closed. "I know you don't want to hear this, but I'm going to say it anyway. Roger did have a point when he brought up the contracts for those gigs. You do have obligations in New Zealand, but it is our home base so I don't think the fans will mind if you take your time with this. But you do have to come back sooner than later – we can't do this without you."

"I know," she agreed as Ryan walked over to her, dragging his luggage on its wheels.

He rested his hands on her shoulders and, staring earnestly at her, added, "I can't imagine everything you're going through but you have to remember, you can't hide away here on this island forever, no matter how tempting that may be. Don't let this grief swallow you whole. You're too good for that and your parents wouldn't want that for you either. The band needs you at home. And I need you at home."

Selene nodded as she held back tears.

"I still need some time," she said, half choking, "but I promise I'll answer when you call."

"What about Roger?"

"Roger, too."

Ryan pulled her in for a tight hug and, with one hand on her neck, held her a moment longer with their noses and foreheads pressed together in the Maori greeting, called hongi. She walked him up the steps to the taxi and waved a limp goodbye as the car sped away.

Chapter Nine

A week had passed since Ryan's departure and Nikos had enjoyed two blissful dates with Selene since then but he felt unusually excited as he drove his motorcycle toward her house that morning. The pressure was on and he knew he had to make the day perfect.

For that day, June 24, marked Selene's twenty-sixth birthday.

Nikos suspected she might feel particularly low and lonely and had been planning a full day for them to spend together since his trip to Athens. He did not want her to be alone on a special day such as this one, and he felt determined to also show her that plenty of things still remained for her to love on the island even though she could no longer enjoy them with her family.

As he parked the bike on the main road and made his way down a path to the pedestrian street and then to the stairs that led to Selene's cavehouse, Nikos went over every detail of his plan, and the anticipation and adrenaline he experienced served as an aphrodisiac. The new couple had taken things slowly in their bourgeoning relationship but it was also Nikos' secret hope that, with all he was about to do for her on her birthday, Selene would finally be ready to fully cross that line from friends to lovers. His body ached for that moment. He had to keep calm though and stay in control of himself – this day was about her, after all. He could wait for the right moment.

With a deep, sobering breath, he crossed her veranda to knock on her door.

* * *

During the early morning hours of Selene's birthday, she awoke excited for the day ahead. She had originally thought her birthday this year would be a quiet, fuss-free affair but, earlier in the week, Nikos had let slip that he had a full day planned for them to enjoy together in celebration, but had refused to divulge the secret itinerary. He wanted each moment to be a surprise for her and she was delighted by his efforts and enthusiasm, which only made her more attracted to him. *How unlikely it is that after all these years and everything that's happened, I am back on this island falling for Nikos – I didn't see that one coming.*

About to hop into the shower, the sound of her phone ringing caused her to detour into the kitchen. Expecting it was Nikos, she raced over to answer it.

"Hey, babe. Happy birthday."

"Oh, it's you," she said flatly. "What do you want, Andrew?"

"Can't a guy call his girl to wish her a happy birthday?"

"Here's the problem with that: I'm not your girl anymore. You fucked up and lost me but can't seem to get that fact through your head."

"Come on, Selene. I'm trying here. Can't you just give me a chance?"

"I could, but I don't want to."

"Selene, I'm begging you. I can't stop thinking about you. I don't think I ever knew how good we had it together until I ruined it. I miss you so much, babe. I wish I was there with you right now for today. If I didn't have to train for a match, I would be. I want to see you. I'll do whatever it takes, but this isn't going to work if it continues over the phone. Can't I just come to the island so we can talk about this in person?"

"No!" she screamed, but then took a deep breath to calm herself. "Andrew, you need to listen to what I'm saying. It's over, and I'm not coming back to you. And talking in person won't help matters either. Even if I could believe you've changed, it's too late anyway. I've started seeing someone else. So that's it. I'm sorry if that's hard for you to hear but it's the truth. I'm trying to move on with my life and I think you should do the same. Now I need to get ready for my day out. Goodbye."

Selene set the phone down on the kitchen table and growled under her breath. *Damn it, Andrew — that's not the way I wanted to start my birthday. Why do you keep haunting me?* She whipped around and headed into the shower.

Twenty calming and steamy minutes later, she emerged and no longer felt huffy. With a towel wrapped around her body as she left the bathroom, Selene walked into her bedroom and hummed to herself as she wove her curls into a long French braid that started above her right ear and curved around the back of her head to end over her left shoulder, leaving a few short pieces out to bounce around her eyes. Then, letting the towel drop to her feet, she slipped into the coral bikini and covered it with her favourite summer dress. It was made of black cotton that was light and soft to the touch, but its details were what made it stand out: the thick halter straps formed a deep V-neck that allowed some of the colour from the bikini top to peak out. The dress was backless to well below her waist, save for a crocheted pattern of swirls that connected the sides up to the middle of her back, with smaller swirls crocheted to the hem just skimming her knees. She finished her outfit with a pair of flat, gold sandals, with straps that criss-crossed over her feet and around her ankles, and a simple pair of gold hoop earrings. Nikos had already told her to leave her purse at home – he planned to treat her to everything that day – so she didn't pack a bag, and was just finishing an application of waterproof mascara and lip gloss when she heard him knock at the door.

As she walked to answer it, one thought crossed her mind: *I hope this outfit does the trick.* For Selene, their last two dates were like hours of foreplay with no finale and her urges had become difficult to control. She knew that Nikos was the gentlemanly type and wanted their first time together to be special so she had decided to play his game, even though she could tell how badly he wanted her. Yet, even after all her teasing touches three nights ago, he had still resisted. *Well, today's my birthday and I want him to be my present even if that means I have to make the first move.* She smirked at that thought and then turned the knob.

Nikos' face said it all when she opened the door: he let his eyes slowly rise from the ground to meet hers, admiring every inch of her, and he had to clear his throat slightly before finally saying, "Selene, you look amazing!"

His hand was nearly shaking as he leaned in, rested it on her cheek and kissed her, but when he tried to pull away she held him there and kissed him again before releasing him. He pulled his face far enough away so only the tips of their noses touched as he added, just louder than a whisper, "And happy birthday."

"Thank you," she replied as he took half a step back and rested his hand on her shoulder.

"Look at this dress on you – so beautiful," he continued as he admired her figure again.

"Well, since I have no idea what you have planned for me today, I had to dress for every possibility. See – even have my bikini on underneath," she pointed out as she playfully fingered one of the straps tied around her neck.

"Perfect. You are ready now?"

"Let me just lock up." And with those five words, Selene slowly turned to close the door, revealing her back to him and she heard him let out a slight gasping grunt at the sight of it. *And the wheels are in motion.* She smiled as she turned the key in the lock.

With his hand resting on the warm, exposed skin of her back, Nikos guided Selene to his motorcycle, slipping her keys into the pocket of his board-shorts as they both mounted the seat. Just before he turned on the ignition, Selene slid her hands around his waist until they wrapped tightly around his torso. She gently rested her chin on his shoulder and asked, "So, where to first?"

"First, we go for a drive. Then a ride on the water."

"You have the boat again?"

"No – better. You will see."

The engine growled as he engaged the key and started them on their journey. The hot summer air smelled fresh and salty and the wind they stirred up as they raced southward along the mountain highway caused their clothing to flap about wildly. Nikos' eggplant-coloured t-shirt inched up above his bellybutton as it moved with the breeze, and Selene used this opportunity to run her fingers over his abs. She had never been on a motorcycle prior to that summer and she loved riding with him, with all of the intimate moments it created for exploitation.

Nikos steered around the tight curves of the hillside as the road took them past the hilltop village of Imerovigli, through the capital of Fira and then on south still until, after nearly thirty minutes, they passed Megalochori, where Nikos pulled over to fill the tank at an old gas station. They stocked up on bottled water, remounted the bike and continued down the road until they reached a fork, where Nikos turned them southeast toward Emporio.

As one of the largest villages on the island, Emporio sat on a low-lying plain framed by hills that made for great hiking. The narrow, almost claustrophobic streets of the village were filled with small homes, hotels and many churches with tall, impressive bell towers. The wind seemed to rush in from the water and over the flat landscape until it hit the rock face that insulated the town, causing the air to swirl around and wander through the crooked corridors between buildings. It added to Emporio's character, already made unique because of Goulas Castle, a remnant of the Ottoman Empire, and the town's ancient marble temple.

Selene had not visited Emporio in years but childhood memories slowly trickled back into her thoughts as they approached Gavrilos hill and its collection of ruined windmills, which were the village's most unique feature. Each windmill was built

Sunsets in Oia

on a small mound fortified by a wall of volcanic rocks set into the soil. Some of the stone cylinders appeared in better condition than others, but none of the eight windmills had been restored to their former glory; instead, they had been abandoned with the passage of time, left to slowly crumble to nothingness along the ridge of the hill. Collections of bright white and yellow daisies grew wildly in the grasses along the ridge and filled the air with a sweet, inviting scent as they danced with the salty sea breeze. Butterflies and honeybees hovered around the petals, feasting on the sweet nectar, and a calico cat with a mixture of black, orange and white fur prowled nearby in search of food.

Nikos parked the motorcycle on the gravel path near the first windmill and guided Selene by the hand further up the hill.

"How are you feeling today?" he asked as they walked along at a leisurely pace, their shoulders rubbing against each other with each step.

"Let's see: it's my birthday and I'm in this gorgeous place with a sexy man on my arm," she replied as she gave his arm a light squeeze and leaned her head on his shoulder. "I've got no worries today. My morning did get off to a rough start though."

"Why?"

"Andrew called, for the second time."

"He still calls you?"

"It turns out the universe has a bit of an ironic sense of humour. His girlfriend just cheated on him and they broke up. But, for some reason, now he claims he can't stop thinking about me. He says he's changed and wants me to give him a second chance."

"What?" Nikos stopped dead in his tracks.

"Don't worry," she said, offering him a reassuring smile. "I blew him off. He doesn't understand that we both have to move on, move forward in our own lives. I know myself enough to say that, even if he truly has changed, I'll never be able to forget what he did to me. I'll just keep turning him down until he gets it."

"That is good," he said, looking down at her with a warm smile as they continued walking, "but I was asking first about your feelings for your family, your house, your music. What about these things?"

"Oh," she exhaled and then became quiet, her eyes glued to her feet as they walked.

"You do not talk much about these things since I came back," he pointed out.

"I know."

"So tell me how you are doing."

"I have good days and bad days," she started. "I've spent a lot of time down by the rock, just playing my guitar."

"This sounds like you feel much better," Nikos offered.

"Yes, I'm playing more now but something still isn't clicking for me. I've got my rhythm back when I play our own songs but it still feels flat to me, like something is missing. I can't figure it out."

"Maybe you play the wrong songs," he suggested simply. "Maybe you try something new and it is better."

"Yeah, maybe." Selene let the idea roll around in her mind for a minute as they walked silently. *Could that be the solution? Should I just start fresh and give something else a try?*

"And I keep returning to my dad's poems. I've read them every single day. It feels like we're sharing something together even though he's gone. I wish we had talked more about his writing before he passed."

"You did not talk to him about this?"

"He sort of kept to himself about it," she recalled. "I just remember him sitting quietly at his desk alone, always deep in thought. He would sort of retreat to that place in his head."

"You are very like him, I think."

"Really – you think so?" Selene pondered this as they continued up the ridge, passing the second mound. "I guess you're right. I retreat into my music in the same way."

"Yes, and you are always thinking, never stopping. Like him."

"Yeah, that's true," she said with a laugh. "We both have trouble turning our brains off. I think that's why he loved coming here so much; the island was his escape."

"He was happy here?"

"Yes. He always seemed happiest here."

"And you?"

"Well, it still feels a bit odd in that house, but I'm stuck with it for now. I heard from Vicky yesterday and that French couple decided to buy a bigger place in Finikia. So much for selling it quickly."

As they approached the third windmill, Nikos led her over to its stone wall and paused to lean against it.

"I think this is a good sign," he said.

"How can it be a good sign that the only interested buyers chose another place?" she asked as she leaned her back against the mound and gazed out at the surroundings.

"Did you really want these people living in your house?"

Selene's chin dropped as she recalled the couple's discussion about renovating the cavehouse, stripping it of everything familiar to her, and she shook her head.

"Honestly? No." she admitted. "They wanted to change everything."

Nikos turned to face Selene and took both of her hands in his.

"I think now you are ready to admit… your house and this place are your escape too," he said as he peered into her eyes. "And like your parents, it is a part of you. You just need a reminder." With that, he released his right hand from her grasp and pointed to a spot on the stone wall. "You see?"

Selene turned her head to look at where he pointed and, after a couple of seconds, she saw it.

"Do you remember?" he asked as the memory came flooding back to her.

There, in that mound, one large rock stood out from the others for its reddish hue and because it displayed her name.

Selene's parents had brought her here with the Kafieris family when she was about twelve years old. As they picnicked on the hill, Selene ran off from the group while Nikos' two sisters played nearby.

"You snuck up behind me that day," she recalled as she ran her finger over the letters, "and you caught me carving my name in the rock. I thought you'd tell on me but you never did." She flashed him a smile and then looked back to the rock, moving her finger along to the carving next to her name.

"You just kneeled down next to me and added your name. They're still here. I can't believe you remembered this."

"You see," he said finally, "you are a part of this place too. That is why you cannot leave."

Selene sighed as she turned to face him and looked deeply into his warm, dark eyes. She wanted to thank him for bringing her back to this spot, for being her rock when she needed one and for reminding her of the deep roots the island had in her entire life, but she did not quite know how to express it. Instead, she cupped his cheek with her small hand, rose up onto her toes and planted a long and loving kiss on his lips.

Placing his hands on her hips with gentle pressure until her back rested against the mound, he leaned forward with the full weight of his body pressed against hers. Selene let out a sensual moan as Nikos' tongue caressed hers and his hands wandered down to stroke her thighs and rear. She lifted one foot and wrapped it around the back of his leg as she slid her hands around to grip the back of his neck, pulling him in even closer. His lips wandered down to her neck for a moment, inspiring her to exhale breathy gasps into his ear, and then his lips returned to hers for one deep, lingering kiss before he suddenly pulled away.

"Come," he said softly and swallowed hard. "We should go."

"But there's no one around and I like it here," she whispered as she ran her fingers through his hair, trying to entice him to kiss her again. But, noticing he would not give in, she asked, "Why? Do you have another surprise waiting for me?"

"Yes," he admitted, "at Perivolos."

As Nikos dropped that clue, he took Selene's hand in his, lightly kissed the skin on the back of it and did not release his gentle grip as he led her back along the ridge to his motorcycle. As they approached the bike, Selene paused and, in a soft voice, said, "Thank you for bringing me back," and gave him a look that suggested she was not just referring to Gavrilos hill and the spot where they had carved their names together in stone. He simply nodded and motioned for them to climb on the motorcycle. With her arms wrapped tightly around his waist once more, they set off down the road heading southeast to the coast.

The village of Perivolos nestled along the water near the southernmost point of the island and remained best known for its expansive and bustling beach, covered in invitingly warm charcoal sand and smooth black stones. Nikos parked the motorcycle on a street that intersected with the long road running parallel to the shoreline, its path obscured from the sparkling azure water only by a row of sparsely spaced trees with narrow, twisting branches and fine leaves. Behind the treeline along the sand stood the occasional pole adorned with a broad canopy thatched together with twigs and thick straw, under which lounged young sunbathers on beach chairs. On the other side of the tree-lined roadway stood a collection of beach pubs, restaurants and shops, and Nikos guided Selene to a nearby building. She noted as they entered that a poster displayed in the window advertised their water activities, snorkeling tours and waterskiing lessons, as well as equipment rentals.

Upon entering the small building, Selene waited near the door while Nikos approached the long counter at the front and, speaking in Greek, told the young man behind it that he had called ahead and made a reservation. He checked Nikos' name off a list, grabbed a set of keys from a peg on the wall behind the counter and led the couple outside. As they approached the water's edge, Selene noticed a small dock in front of them, to which the company had tied three identical Sea-Doos. The sight of them caused a wide grin to spread across her face.

"Did you seriously do this?" she asked.

"A woman should have fun on her birthday," he suggested with a smirk as he accepted the key from

Sunsets in Oia

the shop's employee and pointed with his chin toward the first Sea-Doo. "But I get to drive."

With that, he threw his leg over the seat, straddled the craft and reached back to help Selene get on. Her hand held his as she pounced onto the back and then she latched onto his broad shoulders. With an excited giggle in her voice, she leaned forward and said, "Go fast. Give me a good ride."

He laughed, turned the key and they bolted out into the waves. Racing away from shore, Nikos did a series of turns as they bounced over the water, and Selene, with one hand hooked under his arm and gripping his chest, leaned back and let her free arm flap in the rushing wind as she yelled a joyous holler of exhilaration. They cried out together when Nikos turned them into a large approaching wave and the Sea-Doo leapt over it, gliding through the air until it bounced back into the water and skidded forward. The salty sea splashed up around them but their speed and the shape of the craft managed to deflect most of the spray.

After about forty minutes, when they were nearly a hundred metres from shore, he slowed the Sea-Doo and brought them to a halt in the open water. Turning his head to Selene, Nikos asked, between deep breaths of excitement, "Are you having fun?"

"Definitely," she said with an enthusiastic nod, "but we're just getting started."

She stood straight up suddenly while still straddling the seat, bent forward slightly and slowly lifted the bottom of her dress up and over her head. Resting it over the handlebar, Selene flashed Nikos a naughty grin and then let out a childlike giggle as she hurdled herself over the edge and into the cool water. Her head bobbed up quickly and she flicked her hands forward as she surfaced to send a splash toward him.

"What are you waiting for? Get in here!" she exclaimed, which stirred Nikos from his seat. He took off his shirt and jumped in after her. She splashed him again as he quickly swam over to her but she could not splash him a third time because he had a hold of her by then. As his powerful legs kicked like an eggbeater at a furious pace to keep him afloat, his hands gripped her hips as he pulled her into him. Her dainty legs limberly wrapped around his waist as she curled her arms around his neck and they hovered there next to the Sea-Doo and shared a lengthy kiss. Yet the moment was not so engrossing that Selene failed to notice Nikos' kicking beginning to slow and their chins inching toward the surface. And then she felt it: despite the cool temperature of the water, the heat of the moment had inspired arousal and Nikos' erection brushed against the underside of her thigh. The feeling of it grazing her skin caused their lips to part and Selene exhaled a gleeful, airy laugh while Nikos let out a boyish grunt that suggested a mixture of embarrassment and longing. Staring at him, Selene loosened her arms from around his neck and allowed her legs to slide down ever so slightly until she held his penis between them – a sensation that stirred an obvious lustful urge in Nikos that she could see in his eyes. But before he could draw her back in for another kiss, she impulsively pulled one hand back and speedily sent a small splash into his face, which made her giggle. He shot her a sly, devious glare and just as suddenly propelled both arms outward with such force that her petite body went flying from his grasp and into the air before splashing down a few feet away. Her mouth gaping open in laughter, she splashed him wildly in response and then quickly made for the Sea-Doo.

"Well, come on then," she shouted back to him as she climbed out of the water and quickly dressed herself. "I'm not done with you yet."

Nikos stroked forward rapidly and as he clambered out of the sea, she playfully shoved his shirt at him and said with a smirk, "And this time, I'm driving." One eyebrow shot up as she turned and settled into the seat with Nikos behind her. His hands slid forward and rested on the tops of her thighs.

"Hold on there, mister —" and with that, the Sea-Doo darted forward as she raced them out further toward a nearby catamaran. Moving as fast as the motor would propel them, Selene turned the craft around the boat in broad circles and then raced toward the shore. She timed it perfectly and they rode a large wave in to within fifteen feet of the beach before she yanked on the handle and aimed them back out to the deeper water again, driving them into the curling and breaking waves as they went. Back in the deep water, Selene spun them around in tight turns the way a downhill skier races around slalom course flags while soaring over the icy surface to the finish line.

A half an hour later, Nikos motioned that they should head in so she pointed them inland and they slowly cruised back to the dock. Nikos tied the Sea-Doo to the wooden post and darted back to the rental office to return the key. Once he returned to her, Selene threw her hands around Nikos' neck and declared, "That was fabulous! What a great birthday surprise!"

She planted a kiss on him, after which he said softly, "And the day is still young. Come — are

Sunsets in Oia

you hungry?"

"Famished!"

Nikos nodded, took her hand and they walked back to their parking spot. The bike roared as they rolled along the beachside road, heading northeast until they reached the adjoining village of Perissa. They continued on the same road all the way into town. Nikos pulled over to the side of the beach-front street and pointed to a restaurant facing the water, named Ntomatini.

"It is a new place," he pointed out. "Used to be a tavern but it has new owners now. Very unique mezé plates, very good food."

As Selene looked over at it, she could tell the place offered a stylish atmosphere and followed a growing trend on the island in which business owners trans-formed their traditional eateries to offer a more classy, Neuvo-Greek gastronomic experience.

An expansive patio facing the water dominated the exterior of Ntomatini, its white wooden panels glistened in the bright light. The occasional vine plant wound its way up the columns supporting the wooden roof, which the owners had also painted white. The place even used tablecloths of simple, white linen, but bright fuchsia table legs poked out from underneath their covers, and all of the chairs around them were painted with an intense lime green colour.

Selene and Nikos walked through the entrance onto the patio, where they were greeted by a man who introduced himself as Kostas, one of the owners. He guided the couple to a nearby table, one of the few empty ones, and asked them for their drink order as he handed them menus. Nikos mentioned they were celebrating Selene's birthday that day and they should definitely have some wine, to which Kostas immediately wished her a happy birthday and said he would bring over a complimentary carafe. A couple of minutes later, he returned with the wine and two glasses and asked for their order.

"May I?" Nikos asked as he turned to Selene.

"Go ahead. It all looks so good."

"Okay," he said and turned back to Kostas. "We will share your vegetable mezé plate and a serving of your stuffed squid."

"Excellent choice. I will return shortly with them. Please enjoy your wine."

As Nikos poured her a glass of wine and one for himself, he raised his gaze long enough to ask her, "So, is this a good birthday so far?"

"It's wonderful. I can't believe you planned all this for me," she gushed.

"It is only half of it. We go to Fira next,"

he revealed.

"Oh really? And what will we do there?"

"I am taking you shopping. The birthday girl needs a birthday present," he said as he raised his glass to toast her. "Anything you want, it is yours. To you."

Their eyes fixed on each other as they clinked the glasses together and took their first sips of the dry, white wine, which possessed an oaky tone and the sweet aftertaste of citrus.

About fifteen minutes later, Kostas returned with their meal, which exceeded their expectations. The mezé plate nearly overflowed with delicious options – zucchini fritters, stuffed tomatoes, marinated capers, sautéed mushrooms and phyllo-wrapped leek and feta rolls – and the chef served the stuffed squid whole, save for the head, and its size made it a meal just by itself. Nikos split the squid onto two plates, handed one to Selene and they helped themselves to the vegetables on the other platter. As they slowly savoured their meal over the next hour, they reminisced about previous summers their families had spent together on the island, and recalled many of the fun-filled stories about her family. It made Selene think of her parents in a wholly positive way for the first time since the funeral. The memories were enough to make her forget their tragic end for those few moments as she smiled and laughed with Nikos and did not even feel tempted to cry. They teased each other about some of the crazy and silly things they did as children and, by the time Kostas returned to remove their empty plates, Selene was finally acting like her usual, bubbly self. Before Kostas returned to the kitchen, though, Selene asked him to bring her a plastic bag, which she took with her into the bathroom.

"I didn't want to be out in a wet suit all day and thought this way at least my dress can dry," she told Nikos upon her return as she held up the plastic bag to show him that it contained her bikini. "Can I put this in the top-box?"

"Of course," Nikos said as he stood. "I will pay and then we can go."

After paying and tipping Kostas, they walked back across the street to his motorcycle.

"Can you open the boot for me?" she asked.

Nikos unlocked it and she quickly tossed the bag with her swimsuit inside the enclosure, secured the hatch and then threw her leg over the back of the bike as Nikos turned the key in the ignition. A light but cooling breeze comforted them and offset the blazing heat of the mid-afternoon sun as they rode along, retracing their earlier drive back to Megalochori and then connecting to the island's highway that would take them north to Fira. As Nikos sped up to pass the occasional truck or ATV caravan, Selene glanced out at the glorious view of the caldera and realized for the first time since arriving on the island that summer exactly how hard it would be to leave. *Buyers aren't exactly rushing to take the cavehouse off my hands. Maybe that means I'm supposed to keep it.* She continued to ponder her situation as her braided curls flapped about her neck in the oncoming wind. Her mind lingered on that possibility and all of the advice offered to her by Nikos, Ryan and Vicky, which kept her silent all the way into the capital.

Nikos pulled off the highway and drove into the centre of Fira, where the streets bustled with activity on that perfect Thursday afternoon. Hundreds of people crowded the downtown district, some walking along in pairs while others moved in groups led by tour guides. Nikos slowly made his way through the traffic toward the markets and managed to park the motorcycle in a small lot, filled with dozens of Vespas, about a block from the bus terminal.

Selene let Nikos take her hand as he guided her up the block and turned them down a narrow corridor flanked by clothing and shoe stores, jewellers and taverns.

"What present do you want?" he asked as they inched their way past store windows in a sea of tourists.

"I don't really need anything," she replied.

"Not something you need," he corrected her. "Get something you want. A dress, nice shoes, jewellery – anything you want."

"Well, I'm certainly spoiled for choice here," she said as her eyes wandered from window to window, looking for something to tempt her.

They paused in the entrance of a few shops and tried on sunglasses together. In one store, using a set of worry beads, Nikos performed a perfect impersonation of his crotchety, old father, causing Selene to burst out laughter. As they reached the end of the block, they slipped into a dessert shop and shared a cup of bacio gelato while seated on a couch in the cozy back corner of the store.

"You know, I could use some new guitar strings. You can buy me those if there's a good music store around here," Selene mentioned as she tried to fight off the brain freeze from the gelato.

"We will go to Nostos. They will have your strings," he said as he offered her the last bite of gelato.

They made their way over to the main street of the shopping district, known as Gold Street for its abundance of jewellery stores. As they neared the storefront for Nostos, Selene paused in front of a window at one of the neighbouring jewellery shops and marvelled at a bracelet on display. Inspired by traditional Byzantine designs, its band was made of braided, silver strands held close together by a decorative clasp to create a cuff nearly three inches wide. A simple locking pin operated as the clasp, hidden between the edges of two identical petals that covered the entire top of the bracelet. Their flat edges faced each other on either side of the pin, and they had a thin border that surrounded an intricate filigree design expertly hammered by hand into the metal. But the most beautiful feature of the piece was the two dolphins, which lay side by side on top of the petals and facing opposite directions. They were missing flukes but their bodies tapered and blended into the corners of the petals, with their eyes made of small pieces of blue-green opal. Selene had never seen a bracelet like it and desperately wanted it for herself.

Selene appeared transfixed, so Nikos asked, "Which is your favourite?"

"They're all so lovely, but I like that dolphin bracelet the best."

"You should try it on," he suggested.

"Oh no, Nikos, that will just make me want it.

Let's just go to the music store."

As they walked forward again toward Nostos, Selene quickly looked back one more time at the bracelet in the window.

The owner of Nostos had made very good use of the available space in his brightly lit but small store. Racks of CDs, mostly of Greek and European music, filled one whole wall from floor to ceiling, with the rest of the store divided into small rows displaying music DVDs, traditional Greek instruments and other gift items. As Selene admired the bouzoukis, lyras and baglamas hanging on the wall and ran her fingers gently along their strings, Nikos announced he felt thirsty and wanted to run out to buy a drink.

"Do you want one too?" he asked as he turned to leave.

"No thanks, I'm fine. I'll just wait here and check out all this stuff."

"Okay. I will be back quickly."

Nearly fifteen minutes later, Selene sat in the corner of the music shop, entranced by the sounds her fingers created on the bouzouki in her lap, when she spotted Nikos returning. He held a bottle of juice in one hand.

"I haven't played one of these in years," she said as he approached her. "I forgot how different they feel

Sunsets in Oia

from guitars."

"Did you find your strings?" he asked.

"Yes. The man is holding them for me at the counter," she replied as she stood and returned the instrument to its place on the wall. "I also picked out a new strap, if you don't mind. Mine's getting worn and they have a nice blue one here in braided leather. I thought it could be my gift, if that's all right with you."

"Of course," he said and kissed her cheek as they headed to the cash register.

Nikos paid for Selene's guitar strings and strap. The shopkeeper handed him the bag, which he passed to Selene.

"For you. The birthday girl gets what she needs," he said just as he pulled a small gift bag out from behind his back, "and what she wants."

Selene looked at the bag and then at Nikos with a frown and pursed her lips. "Where did this come from?"

"Open and you will see."

Selene pulled a large square box from inside the bag and her eyes went wide with wonder when she removed the lid to reveal the dolphin bracelet.

"I came back with more than juice," he admitted. "Do you like it?"

Her eyes bulging, Selene could only nod her head

as she stared at the gift. Nikos reached in and pulled it out of the box, delicately slid the pin out, slipped the bracelet on her wrist and returned the pin to its slot to lock the bracelet in place.

"Beautiful," he whispered, as he cradled her dainty hand in his and stared at the bracelet for a moment. "It suits you."

As his eyes rose to meet hers, she lifted the hand now framed by his gift and pressed it against his cheek, leaned forward on her toes and kissed him. The man behind the counter watched as they lingered before him, lip-locked, until Selene finally pulled away.

"Thank you. I can't believe you did this," she said as they left the store holding hands. "I'll wear it every day."

At about seven o'clock, the downtown crowd began to thin as the tour groups returned to the docking area below the city to be tendered back to their cruise ships anchored in the caldera. Other visitors, hungry from shopping and sight-seeing, abandoned the streets for the comforts of a table with a view and tasty local cuisine in various nearby restaurants. Nikos and Selene made their way back to his motorcycle, put their bags in its top-box and headed back onto the road leading to Oia. As they sped along, Selene gripped Nikos tightly and pressed up against his back as much as possible to steal his body heat while the evening breeze gave her a bit of a chill.

At the halfway point on the road to the village, Nikos pulled the bike off the highway and stopped at a roadside cabana.

"I remember this place," Selene said as they approached it. "We'd stop here for a drink and rest when we used to go tramping on the mountain trail. I'm surprised it looks so quiet; this place was always so busy."

The dingy structure looked no bigger than a trailer home, with two small canopies erected next to it on metal poles to provide shelter for the few sets of available patio seating. Nikos parked the motorcycle just off the road next to the cabana and told Selene they would stop to watch the sunset.

"Right here?" she asked. "But it won't set for nearly an hour."

"Not here," he said, correcting her. "Up there on the hill. It is the best view." He pointed up the nearby path to the top of Megalo Vouno, a vast but isolated mountain that rose up along the edge of the cliff and looked out to the caldera. Its steep edges towered over them and ended at a height that made it one of the highest peaks on the island. The dirt path snaked its way to the summit.

Selene held Nikos' hand as he led her up the narrow path at a slightly hurried pace and, when they reached the highest point along the path, he guided her away from the trail a short distance until he found a flat section of rock that formed a natural seat. As they sat down close together, they took in the beauty of the panoramic view before them. The wind offered the only sound and the air was especially clear, allowing them to observe the entire west-facing curve of Santorini as well as outlines of a few of the neighbouring islands within the Cyclades group. The sun crept down, preparing for the big show, and the sky above it began to fade from its usual brilliant blue into pale shades of mauve and amber. Selene felt Nikos' warmth when he wrapped his arm around her as they sat in silence and watched as the great orb inched lower. As its bottom lip dipped below the watery horizon, she thought about her father's poem and how much that moment must mirror so many others her parents had shared together. She pulled her gaze away from the sunset just long enough to glance over at Nikos and, when his eyes met hers, she flashed him a sweet smile and lightly kissed him. Their eyes settled on the sunset once more as they watched the last glimpse of the fireball disappear into the waves.

"We must go," Nikos said a minute later. "The

path will get too dark if we wait."

They made their way quickly and carefully down the mountain. The sky rapidly faded from a vibrant dance of colours to blackness and the first of the stars began to twinkle above them. Selene paused, tilted her head back and smiled as she admired them before she turned to Nikos.

"So, is dinner our next stop?" she asked him.

"Yes," he said as he reached into his top-box and pulled out his cell phone to send a quick text message. "We must hurry now."

With that, he returned his phone to its storage place and they raced around the mountain and back into Oia. The village looked alight with a greenish-white glow, which was mostly produced by the bevy of expensive hotels and their well-lit grounds and pools. Outside of Oia, the only visible light came from the closest adjacent towns and the few scattered properties lining the coast on the flat land below the rise. Otherwise, the island and the horizon were lost to the shadowy night. Nikos parked the motorcycle in a small lot around the corner from Bougainvillea and when they walked in the front door of the restaurant, Stefanos was waiting for them. Selene noticed he had not dressed in his uniform that evening, but she didn't think anything of it in that moment.

"Is everything ready?" Nikos asked him in Greek in a low tone, to which Stefanos nodded and hurried them upstairs. As they walked through the glass doorway to the rooftop patio, Selene was greeted by a rousing cheer from Nikos' parents, his sisters Emmelia and Larissa, uncle Pavlo, his cousin Dimitris from Fira and even Vicky and her fiancé, Gabriel. Selene's jaw dropped as she looked at the table full of her loved ones and her heart swelled for the man standing next to her who had arranged it all.

"I can't believe you did all this for me!" she said as she looked up at him.

"I mentioned it to Emmelia when I saw her in Athens so she had Larissa come with her. Everyone else already lives here. Come say hello."

Selene greeted all of the guests before she took the seat at the head of the table, with Nikos sitting to her right. Stefanos joined the party too and claimed the empty chair next to his father. As they all got settled, Spiro arrived with a large bottle of champagne, which he poured into everyone's flute glasses. Before anyone could take a sip, Pavlo insisted that Selene make a speech. The whole table started to shout out in agreement and encouraged her until, with her cheeks blushing, she stood up.

"I haven't made a very big deal of my birthday

Sunsets in Oia

for many years," she said with a unsteady smile as she swallowed hard and tried to keep herself from tearing up, "but I've never been alone on this day either. I've always had family or friends around to make it special. And now, with everything that's happened…it's so lovely to see you all here to help keep that tradition alive." Selene raised her glass of champagne and looked around at each face at the table. "A toast to all of you: thank you for coming and making a wonderful day even better. Cheers!"

Everyone raised their flutes and a chorus of "Opa!" sounded as the glasses met and filled the air with a high-pitched jingling ring. Selene sat down again, leaned over to Nikos, kissed his cheek and whispered, "Thank you for this." As she stared into his dark eyes, Pavlo interrupted their moment when his rough hand landed on her shoulder.

"We have prepared a feast for you, my dear," he exclaimed as she turned to face him. He shouted to Spiro, standing off to the side, to bring up the food. Spiro nodded to his boss and hurried down the stairs toward the kitchen. When Spiro returned moments later, two other waiters and one of the chefs followed him.

"Oh my god – look at all the food," Selene gasped.

Each man balanced a large tray on his shoulder, which carried platters of food for the birthday feast.

They featured a great mixture of mezés, including tomato fritters, dolmades and olives with cheese, as well as large servings of okra in a tomato sauce with potatoes and shredded lamb, spaghetti with lobster, grilled swordfish, and chicken breasts stuffed with spinach and feta with grilled zucchini on the side. As the men placed the dishes in the middle of the table for the party, another young server with shaggy hair appeared, carrying a tray of four bottles of wine from one of the island's wineries and enough tumblers for everyone at the table.

The feast stretched over nearly two hours as everyone took turns telling jokes and stories, and by the end they had the entire rooftop patio to themselves. As everyone slowly consumed the last bites of the exquisite meal and leaned back in their chairs, Pavlo stood and announced that, even though they had now closed the restaurant, the party was just getting started. He took off for downstairs, which prompted Stefanos to leave the table with him.

When Pavlo returned to the rooftop patio carrying the dessert platter, he wasn't alone. Eight other staff members followed father and son upstairs, half of whom carried musical instruments, which they set up on the small stage in the corner and then they cleared some floor space for dancing. Meanwhile, Pavlo presented the party with the sweets, which

included baklava, apple-cinnamon pie, and miniature chocolate raspberry cakes. Stefanos added two
bottles of vinsanto and a bottle of Ouzo with plenty
of cordial glasses to go around.

Then the music began. Pavlo and Stefanos joined
Spiro and Loukas, one of the chefs, on the stage.
Pavlo led them on the bouzouki and laouto, with
Stefanos on an acoustic guitar, Spiro playing a violin
and Loukas banging on a toubeleki drum. Their
performance of popular songs by such renowned
Greek musicians as Markos Vamvakaris, Yiannis
Parios, George Dalaras and Giorgos Zampetas
prompted the other employees to get up and dance.
Selene watched as the scene inspired a youthful
energy to bubble up in Sophia as she jumped out
of her chair and encouraged everyone at the table
to join in the fun. More tables were pushed toward
the walls as the dancing line grew while Georgios
sat off to the side watching and tapping his cane on
the floor with a great grin on his face. Nikos and his
cousin Dimitris, who were the strongest dancers
in the group, took turns leading the line and doing
various solo moves, for which they earned cheers
from everyone. Selene watched Nikos as he nimbly
moved about, twisting and turning, kneeling down
and leaping into the air.

After many songs, there was a break in the music

and Pavlo called for Selene to join him on the stage.

"You did not sing for us last time," he shouted out to her. "Pick a song for us now."

For the first time since she lost her parents, Selene did not hesitate as she broke free from the dancing line and ran over to the platform to join the band. She already knew which song she wanted to sing and her favourite version of it had been recorded by Mariza Koch, one of her mother's favourite Greek singers.

"Do you guys know 'Kapetan Andrea Zeppos?'" she asked. The men all nodded.

Even without a microphone, Selene's beautiful voice rose up above the instruments and delivered a playful and energetic rendition. The guests did not resume dancing but instead stood and listened in awe as Selene performed in public for the first time since her parents were killed. The experience felt invigorating and Selene smiled all the way through it. Once the song ended, Nikos started the group in a round of applause, and they called out for her to sing another tune.

"I think I'd rather break open that Ouzo," she declared. "Who's with me?"

Everyone joined in and, after a couple rounds of shots, they had emptied the bottle and the dancing resumed, continuing for another hour before some of the older guests decided to call it a night. As Selene thanked everyone for the wonderful birthday party and saw them off, Nikos helped Pavlo and Stefanos carry the dishes down to the kitchen. Once they were the last guests remaining, they thanked their hosts and walked out of the restaurant.

As they slowly made their way back to the motorcycle, both of them stumbled slightly over the uneven ground, which was influenced more by all of the drinks consumed at dinner. Selene felt Nikos' arm slip around her waist as they talked about how much fun they had that day. They rode the bike a short distance and parked along the main road next to St. George's Church on the other end of the village. From there, she led him by the hand down the nearby steps that would take them to her cavehouse, but when they reached the spot where it curved to the right, she continued down the steps past the walkway leading to her veranda.

"Where are we going?"

"You'll see," she replied as she glanced back at him, flashing him a giddy smile. "It's your turn for a surprise."

After a few minutes, they reached the end of the path and walked onto the small strip of beach where they had gone swimming with Ryan. The clear night sky glistened with thousands of brilliant stars and the high-hanging full moon illuminated the waves as they crashed against the shore. They kicked off their sandals and walked barefoot along the dark, cool sand.

"I can't remember the last time I had so much fun," she admitted as she slowly turned to face him. "I still can't believe you planned that whole day for me."

"You are worth it," he said softly as he pulled her in for a long, wet kiss.

When Selene finally pulled away, she took a few short paces back and, with her eyes fixed on him, said, "The night is still young. Let's go swimming."

"But you bikini is still in my trunk," he replied, a big grin on his face.

"I know."

With her confidence fueled by the alcohol in her system, Selene gripped the sides of her dress and slowly pulled it all the way up and over her head. Then she lowered her arms to her sides again, letting the dress drop to the sand as she stood before him. Nikos' mouth parted slightly as he stared at her. The soft moonlight highlighted her delicate shoulders, round and perky breasts, narrow waist, curvy hips and long, slender legs. She casually turned and headed into the cool water, but once the waves started to meet her hips she turned back to face him.

Sunsets in Oia

"Aren't you going to drop your gear and join me?"

Smiling, he quickly stripped off his clothes and raced in after her. His enthusiasm made her feel giddy and she let out a giggle as he reached her and pulled her into his arms. The waves steadily broke just below his shoulders as he scooped her up and planted a deep and heavy kiss on her lips. With one arm wrapped around his neck and the other hand gripping his wet hair, she pulled herself up and wrapped her legs tightly around his waist. His strong hands softly stroked her back and slowly slid down to grip her buttocks. As Nikos' tongue caressed hers, his hands pushed her hips down slightly until the tip of his long, hard member could feel the warm, wet opening between her legs. Selene let out an erotic gasp as she felt his penis thrust inside her in one swift motion, and their lips stayed locked together as they began to make love in the water.

And then the wave hit them.

They had been so wrapped up with each other that they didn't see it coming. Much bigger than those that had preceded it, the wave rushed up from behind them and knocked Nikos off his feet, sending both of them under the surface and pulling Selene from his grasp. She made a bee-line for the shore and was emerging from the sea by the time Nikos' head breached again. Selene giggled as she looked back and saw him wipe the salty sea from his eyes and spot her naked figure running on the beach. She squeezed some of the water out of her braid; the rest of the seawater beaded on her dark skin, reflecting the moonlight in a way that made her glow, like a mythical sea nymph emerging from her home to tempt one of the island's men.

"Come on, Nikos!" she called out. She watched as he ran toward the shore, his feet slipping over the rocky sea bed as the waves pounding the back of his calves threw him off-balance. By the time he reached the sand, Selene had already scooped up her dress, slipped her feet into her sandals and was racing up the rocky path, sliding the dress over her head as she went. She glanced back and saw Nikos hurriedly pulling his black boxer-briefs and sandals on, tossing his other clothes over his shoulder as he chased her up the cliffside.

Selene possessed great agility as she leapt up the uneven steps, and had nearly reached her veranda by the time Nikos caught up with her. She could hear him coming up behind her as she reached the walkway. She turned around just in time for him to slip his hands around her waist and lift her off her feet again. Nikos carried her as their chests heaved together and his lips wandered from her shoulder, up her neck and then met her perfect pout. When he reached the front door, Nikos pushed Selene's back up against it and leaned into her, causing her to feel his mighty bulge press against her thighs again.

"I have to have you now. Where are my keys?" she asked breathlessly between his kisses. Nikos pulled the shorts off his shoulder and fumbled them in the dark until he found the zippered pocket. When he handed the key ring to her, she whipped around and quickly opened the door.

Within seconds of getting inside the house, Nikos pulled Selene's dress over her head and ran his hands over her soft skin as he kissed her, all the while slowly guiding her through the main room to the first bedroom. When the backs of her legs met the edge of the bed, Selene slowly kneeled down, kissing Nikos' chest and abs as she pulled down his damp and sandy underwear. As she caressed his throbbing shaft with her dainty hands, her tongue licked and teased its tip until she slid it into her mouth, drawing a pleased groan from Nikos as he watched her intently.

After a few minutes, he suddenly gripped her shoulders and pulled her up to her feet and then lightly pushed her back onto the bed. As Selene spread her legs open for him, he climbed on top of her, running the tip of his tongue along her stomach and then teased her nipples as he inched forward.

Nikos' hands tightly gripped Selene's hips as she lifted her legs and wrapped them around his buttocks. Her back arched and she let out a moan as his cock slipped deep inside her. His movements were slow and steady initially. Their lovemaking ebbed and flowed as they teased each other to new heights of rapture. As Selene became increasingly wet and her moaning spurred him on, Nikos' animalistic urges took over. They rolled around the bed in a sweaty, orgasmic embrace that continued for over an hour.

Once they climaxed together, Nikos wrapped Selene in his arms and pulled her down next to him. She nestled her head in his shoulder as he cradled her back with one arm.

"That was perfect," he whispered as he brushed damp strands of hair from her face with the tip of his finger.

"So is this." Her voice sounded soft and breathy, and her eyes glistened as she looked at him and started to run her fingers through his tuft of dark, curly chest hair. Their comforting embrace and intense body heat, along with the repetitive stroking motion of her hand, quickly lulled both of them to sleep.

Chapter Ten

The next morning, Selene's nose woke first as the familiar and stirring scent of freshly brewed coffee enticed it. As her eyes slowly parted to be greeted by the light, she saw a hand holding a coffee mug.

"What time is it?"

"Nearly nine," Nikos replied softly. "I made this for you. I would like to start breakfast."

She sat up halfway, took the mug and then glanced at her surroundings.

"Oh, we slept in here all night?"

"Yes," he said as he stood. "You slept first and you were smiling." He motioned toward the kitchen. "Are you hungry?"

"I have to get out of this bed," she stated dryly as she abruptly threw back the sheet and stood up. Noticing she was still naked, Selene rushed over to the wardrobe, pulled her mother's robe off its hanger and wrapped herself in it.

"You slept late," Nikos added as he watched her. "Let me fix you some eggs."

"No," she blurted out, "you don't understand. We shouldn't have been in their room. It was a mistake."

Nikos crossed his arms and frowned. "I do not understand."

"This is their bed," she pointed out. "That crossed a line."

He nodded as he looked down at his feet but then shook his head, and when his eyes rose to meet hers again they looked dark and angry.

"Selene, they are gone."

"It still feels wrong to me being in here," she admitted.

"This does not stop you last night."

"I know, but... Ugh, it's too hard to explain!" The words stumbled out of her mouth as she struggled to find the right ones.

"No, Selene, it is simple," he insisted.

"You still don't get it! I can't just move on, Nikos," she blurted back in a shaky voice. "You have no idea what I'm going through!"

Nikos threw up his hand to stop her, staring harshly into her eyes. "You live in the past with your ghosts. I will not." He pushed his hair back with his hand and hurried out of the room.

"Where are you going?" she called as she followed him into the main room to find him heading for the door. Selene pulled on his arm and he turned back to her with a sombre and defeated look in his eyes.

"I know what I want, Selene, but you do not. Until you do, I cannot be here."

Nikos turned and walked out the door. She called out after him but he did not turn around. Tears welled up in her eyes as she stepped to the small kitchen table, leaned over it for a moment and then slammed the coffee cup down on its surface. The mug teetered and fell over, spilling its contents over the table and the hot, black liquid quickly absorbed into most of the sheets of paper, her father's hand-written poems, which she had spread out days before over half of the tabletop. Selene tried to pick them up but they started to tear apart between her fingers. She rushed over to the counter and grabbed a cloth in a desperate attempt to soak up the spill but it did little to salvage the pages or prevent the ink from running. On many of the papers, her father's beautiful words and clean penmanship had been reduced to illegible smudges. Selene delicately held them in her hands and stared at what her anger had destroyed. Her knees buckled as she collapsed on the floor and cried. Her entire body shook uncontrollably with the wailing and she pulled her legs up tight against her chest. As a few of the destroyed poems lay in a wasted heap at her feet, Selene tried to control her breathing while still curled in the fetal position, her face pressed tightly into her knees, but by that point her powerful sobs were bordering on hyperventilation.

Many minutes passed before Selene finally steadied herself and lifted her head. As she wiped the tears from her blotchy face, her reddened eyes opened and the first thing she saw was her old guitar resting in her father's chair as it slowly rocked back and forth.

* * *

On late Saturday morning, the air felt cool. A thick and low-hanging patch of cloud covered much of the sky, blocking the heat and light of the summer sun. Selene sat outside at a table with Vicky. She needed a girlfriend to talk to and Vicky was really the only one she had on the island. They met at Melenio Café and overlooked the caldera as they awaited the

Sunsets in Oia

arrival of their meals. Vicky remained quiet.

"I'm guessing you're wondering why I asked you here this morning," Selene began as she sipped her coffee.

"I was a bit surprised," Vicky admitted. "You sounded quite upset on the phone."

"It's Nikos," Selene said. "We spent the night together after my party."

"Oh! Good for you, honey. You two make such a good couple. But why so sad?" Vicky asked.

"It was so incredible and then I ruined it. We had a fight the next morning and he stormed out."

Vicky frowned at her. "Why did you fight if it was so great?"

"I got upset because we spent the night in my parents' bed. It made me feel weird, as though I had dishonoured them, and Nikos just didn't understand. He wants me to move on from my loss but thinks I'd rather live in the past with their ghosts. But it's not that simple to me. He was right about one thing though: I don't know what I want. I feel so stuck, Vicky, and I could use your advice. I don't know what to do about him or the house or anything right now."

Vicky nodded but, just as she was about to respond, Selene's phone, sitting on the corner of the table, began to vibrate. She glanced down and noticed the Caller-ID read Roger's name and number.

"I'm sorry, but I have to take this. It's my manager."

"Go ahead," Vicky nodded.

"Hi, Roger. What's up?"

"Gidday, dear. Sorry to bother you, but we've got a problem over here."

She frowned. "What's wrong?"

"I've been getting calls all day from journalists about you and these new photos."

"What photos?"

"Someone there on the island recognized you and snapped a bunch of shots of you at the beach on a Sea-Doo with some guy. The photographer sold three shots to The Herald, which ran yesterday. I'm looking at it now: there's one of you two on the Sea-Doo, another of this guy tossing you into the air and then the two of you kissing."

"Oh, no."

"That's not the worst of it," he continued. "The headline's a real piece of work. Over the pictures in big, block letters, it says, 'Where's the grief?' And then under that is the caption: 'Kauri Spirit front-woman Selene Doherty celebrates her birthday with a mystery man on the Greek island of Santorini. The Wellington-based band has been on hiatus since the tragic deaths of Doherty's parents last month in Athens while she claimed to be hiding out in mourning in the Mediterranean.'"

"Holy shit!" she said loud enough to draw the gaze of patrons at nearby tables.

"That's what I said when I first saw it," Roger added. "Now I've got editors from rags all over the country and in Australia and the States calling me to confirm this story and wanting the name of this man of yours. What the hell is going on over there?"

"Are you asking for the editors or yourself, Roger?"

"Look, love, if you want to keep this thing quiet, that's your decision. But it's all over the web and the bloggers are going nuts over this. Now, I've talked to Ryan and all he would tell me is that you've been seeing this guy for a little while. What and who you do isn't my business. But considering the situation with the tour and what happened with your family, this doesn't look good. I don't mean to pile on; I just want you to be aware. What do you want me to do?"

Selene paused for a moment and then said, "If they keep calling, just say I refused to comment."

"You really wanna stay quiet on this?"

"Yes."

"I know you don't want me to ask, but I have to: what about the tour?"

"I'm still trying to sort out issues here with the house," she explained. "I'm sorry, Roger, but the tour's going to have to wait a bit longer."

"All right," he said with a sigh. "I'm not happy about this but I'm going to trust you on this one. I don't want to get blindsided like this again. At least these shots of you look great and you seem happy in them. I'm glad that's the case. Ryan told me you've really been struggling with your situation and asked that I not pressure you so much. I know you think I acted like an insensitive jerk last time and I'm sorry for that. This whole situation has all of us stressed but I'll get us through it one way or another. Gotta go, love, but hurry home soon. We miss you over here."

"Okay. Thanks, Roger."

As Selene hung up the phone, she shook her head but then realized how much worse it could have been. *If that damn photographer had followed us to the beach that night, then I'd have a real scandal on my hands – even worse than when the shit hit the fan with Andrew.*

"Is everything okay?" Vicky asked.

"Not exactly," Selene admitted. "A photographer took some shots of me and Nikos together at the beach on my birthday and sold them to the press back home." Her phone beeped for a text message, which turned out to be Roger sending the web address to the story. "And now Roger's sending me the link to them, as if I'd want to see."

"I do!" Vicky reached over and grabbed the phone. Before Selene could steal it back, Vicky clicked on the link and checked out the photographs. "Oh, Selene, you look beautiful in these shots."

"Really?"

"Of course. You have nothing to worry about, except maybe this tasteless headline," she admitted.

"I know – Roger told me," Selene sighed as she sank back into her chair. "Even if the photos look good, that's not exactly going to help my situation with Nikos. How am I going to resolve this?"

Vicky's brow furrowed as she set down the phone and leaned forward, resting her arms on the table.

"You want my advice?" she asked.

"Please," Selene begged. "I'm desperate here."

"Okay," Vicky started. "My boss would fire me if he heard this, but I speak as your friend. I think inside you truly do not want to sell the house. I see it in your eyes with the French couple. And Nikos is right. You are haunted with ghosts. But you do not have to choose between them and him; you can have both. I think that your – what is the word? – perspective needs the makeover."

"A makeover?"

"Yes," Vicky continued. "This place makes you happy. I can see it. But you worry that to move on you will lose your family. If you want to keep their spirits with you, you must honour them. They gave you the house, so keep it and make it for you. And keep Nikos too because they want you to be happy. Let them inspire and help you and you will have all of them with you forever."

"A makeover." Selene considered the suggestion again and, as the waiter delivered their breakfast to the table, Selene's mind flashed back to the sight of her guitar in her father's chair. Her eyes widened. *Vicky's right. They can be my inspiration, the push forward I've been waiting for.*

"A makeover – it's perfect," she said. "I have an idea, Vicky, and you're the ideal person to help me."

Chapter Eleven

Nikos woke alone in his own bed and, as soon as he sat up, he felt filled with a sense of dread. Two weeks had passed since he fought with Selene and stormed out of her house. He had not seen or heard from her since that day. A part of him still felt upset over how she had dismissed his feelings for the sake of her dead parents – even though she was technically still in the dark about how strong his feelings for her happened to be. Now he feared their argument had turned into the catalyst that would tear them apart permanently. He couldn't lose her after all the years he had secretly loved her, especially now that they had finally come together and it felt more perfect than he had ever imagined.

Though the hour seemed early and Selene would likely still be in bed, Nikos rushed into his kitchen and picked up his phone. But as he pushed the buttons, some impulse stopped him and his hand returned the phone to its spot on the wall. Shaking his head, he walked back to the bathroom, stripped off his underwear and stepped into the shower, allowing the cool water to calm him.

However, this soothing part of his morning routine was quickly interrupted only a minute later when his phone began to ring. His ears detected its sound above the trickling water so he turned his shower off and, still dripping wet and naked, rushed out to the kitchen again and snatched the receiver on the fourth ring.

"Nai."

"Hi, Nikos. It's Selene."

"Ah, good morning," he said as calmly as he could. "I am surprised it is you."

"I know. We haven't talked for a while."

"Two weeks," he reminded her. "I started to think we are done and you left."

"No, I'm still here, and I'm so sorry about the fight. I feel awful about what I said and how I treated you, but I needed that time to sort through everything. Are you free today? I was hoping you could come by the house so we can talk."

Nikos couldn't believe his luck – she wanted him back – but he decided to play it with a bit of non-chalance and levity, despite his earnest desire to rush over to her that very minute.

"I have some things to do this morning, Selene, but I can stop in this afternoon maybe. Is around two okay?"

"That's perfect, Nikos, and thank you. I'll see you this afternoon."

"Okay, bye."

Her words echoed in his head and he waited to hear her hang up, staring at his phone for a moment before placing it back in its cradle. His hand continued to rest on it though and he pressed the other palm against the wall, leaning forward and drawing in a few deep breaths. Testosterone rushed through him as his heartbeat quickened its pace. He needed another cold shower.

The morning dwindled away at an agonizingly slow pace as Nikos passed the time buying groceries and doing a few chores – things that easily could have waited for another time. Then, as he watched the clock on his wall finally approach two o'clock, he took a deep breath, locked his door and left to walk to Selene's house. Nikos reached Oia and slowly wove his way through the crowd along the busy pedestrian street, veering to his left when he reached the steps leading down the escarpment. Within only a few feet, the noise of the town above faded away and was replaced by the whirling wind and the clacking of his flip-flops against the stairs. After a few more paces, however, a distant song began to rise up with the breeze to greet him, growing steadily louder with each step he took down the cliffside. By the time he passed his parents' house, he could discern the smooth strumming of an acoustic guitar and a voice that sounded unmistakably like Selene's. As he reached the point where his feet were level with the roof of her cavehouse, he stopped and listened to her and quickly realized the words she sang belonged to her father's poem, "Sunsets in Oia."

She did it, he thought as he watched her play to herself on her veranda while facing the caldera. *She found her inspiration.*

Nikos stood on the step, motionless and silent, as he listened to the rest of the song. He marvelled at the way Selene had adapted the poem into lyrics for a ballad, building up slowly with intensity and highlighting the melody with intricate string work reminiscent of the classic laïkó folk songs of Greece. Her voice rose in pitch and volume as she repeated the final two lines three times in a sort of climactic

Sunsets in Oia

chorus that sounded so painfully beautiful it gave Nikos goose bumps. When Selene struck the final note, she allowed it to ring and fade away into the wind as she lowered her head. After a moment's pause, Nikos called out to her from his position on the stairs.

* * *

"Bravo, my dear." The words broke the lingering silence.

Selene smiled, turned and spotted Nikos just above her adjacent to her house.

"How long have you been standing there?"

"Long enough to hear your beautiful new song," he said as he walked down the last few steps and joined her on her veranda. "This was your father's poem I read."

"That's right. The craziest things have been happening to me, Nikos," she said as she turned to face him, a broad smile lighting her face. "After our fight, I felt really upset and confused but it was something Vicky said that helped everything finally click in my head. Ever since, I've been writing like mad. I've turned three of dad's poems into songs and have written five new compositions of my own. I've decided I want to do a solo album of world folk music inspired by my parents and their Greek, Celtic and Maori backgrounds."

"This is very different from Kauri Spirit," Nikos pointed out.

"I know," she agreed, "but I feel like I've finally found my voice, as if my parents are leading me to it. I have to take what they've given me and embrace it as my own. It all makes sense now. I keep hearing all of the other sounds in my head – the bouzouki, the fiddle, the mandolin, the wailing voice of a Maori chant, the rolling drums, the eerie flutes – it's finally meshing together. It all seems so easy now, and so much of it goes back to what you said to me."

Nikos beamed upon hearing this news. "I am very happy for you," he offered.

"There's more," she continued. "I've been meeting with your uncle, Pavlo, who's helping me by writing the bouzouki parts. I'm going to pitch the solo album to Warner's world music division and, if they buy it, I want to ask Pavlo to record with me. I can't think of anyone better on the bouzouki. Do you think he'd like that?"

"Ah, yes. He always wanted to be a musician. He will say yes, of course," Nikos said as he took her hand in his. "I am proud of you, Selene. You look so happy and in peace."

"I am," she nodded. "Thank you."

"For what?" he asked quizzically.

"For telling me what I needed to hear."

She offered him a sweet and soft smile, her bright green eyes inviting him in as their lips met. When they parted a moment later, Nikos exhaled a sigh of relief and exhilaration as he smiled and gazed down at her.

"I worried very much," he admitted in a sombre tone. "You do not speak to me for two weeks. I think maybe we are done. This was a terrible thought for me. I'm sorry to upset you. I wanted to be here for you."

"I know you didn't mean it," she offered. "It was my fault. I wasn't ready for all this. I just needed some time."

"You are better now?"

"Yes, very much," she nodded. "Come on, let me prove it to you. I have something to show you."

She set the guitar down on the table and led him into the house. When she opened the front door, his eyes widened and his jaw dropped.

Selene had completely remade the house to suit her personal tastes.

The main room had been painted a calming, pale powder blue, and the antique walnut loveseat now had new fabric on its cushions, an azure background with a pattern of vine leaves in a seafoam green shade. Her father's old rocking chair looked revived after being stripped and refinished but Selene had opted to otherwise leave it the same. The bookshelf along the wall had been replaced by a long walnut shelving unit that rose to waist height and housed stereo equipment behind its central glass door, above which sat a new flat-screen television and small speakers. Cora's bronze sculpture of Santorini sat to the right of the television and Frank's book collection filled the two shelves below it. A large, framed poster of an ancient Minoan fresco depicting dolphins swimming in the Aegean hung on the back wall above the rocking chair, and a collage of framed photographs of her family, friends and the band, which formed the shape of a wave, covered most of the wall space above the loveseat. Below it on the floor rested a new Turkish silk rug with a dark blue background and a pattern of white flowers and leaves.

"I still need some art for the wall to the left of the TV," Selene said as Nikos stood in the centre of the room and gazed around him, "but what do you think?"

"You do all this in only two weeks?" he asked.

"I figured that, if I'm going to keep this house, I have to give it a makeover to really make it mine instead of a shrine to my parents."

Nikos turned to face her. "You are keeping it?" he asked.

"Yes," she said, as she walked over to him and held his hands. "I realized I couldn't leave this place, so I've decided to split my time between New Zealand and here. It's not going to be easy, but I know now it's what I really want. I love this place too much to leave it."

As he looked down at her, Nikos let out a deep sigh and his lips curled into a broad smile. "This makes me very happy," he said, but just as he attempted to lean over to kiss her again she stepped away and pulled him forward.

"Come on," she insisted, "I have more to show you."

She led him to the back of the house to the two closed bedroom doors.

"I still haven't updated the kitchen or the bathroom but I'm going to leave that until next year. I finished the bedrooms, though. First: the guest room..." she said as she opened the door on the right, her old room.

Selene had painted the walls a silvery-grey shade. A new double bed with a wrought-iron frame stood against the right wall, covered in a white quilt with a large Greek key pattern in navy blue. A matching iron bedside table sat on the far side of the bed with a small lamp on it. The old dresser from the other room had been stripped, painted black and now leaned against the back wall. A new navy leather chaise longue angled into the room from the opposite corner and a large framed mirror hung next to it.

"What do you think?" Selene asked him curiously.

"It is so different!" he said in awe.

Selene took his hand then and led him out into the hall to the other closed door, that of her parents' old room.

"And now, the grand finale: my new boudoir…" she said as she turned the knob and pushed in the door.

The walls were a pale, rosy coral colour, with the left wall dominated by the old brass-framed queen bed. It looked freshly polished and now bore a large canopy of sheer white linen flecked with gold, draping down from the ceiling above the head of the bed and tucked behind the posts. Bright white sheets with gold embroidered trim and a rich, burgundy duvet covered the mattress, folded down just below the plump pillows. On either side of the bed sat two matching tables with glass tops and black marble legs, on which perched identical black ceramic lamps with buttercream shades that released a soft and warm light into the room. Her parents' old wardrobe still dominated the front wall and her father's antique rolltop desk had a new home in the

Sunsets in Oia

back-right corner of the room. A newly purchased, nineteenth century bench seat sat between them on the wall facing the bed, and its carved oak frame featured off-white cushions with gold trim. Finally, an oversized wooden-framed mirror, which rested on the floor and nearly reached the ceiling, leaned into the back left corner, reflecting the end of the bed and much of the front of the bedroom.

Nikos walked toward the foot of the bed and whistled.

"It is beautiful, Selene," he finally said. "How do you do all this in only two weeks?"

"With help, of course," she said with a laugh. "I did all of the painting and I had Vicky's friend, Penelopi, help with the rest. She's an interior decorator from Athens and she also restores old furniture. She located all of the new pieces for me, found buyers for the stuff I was selling and also refinished the pieces that required repairs or updating. I was amazed by how fast she completed the project but I did pay her for a quick makeover. I'm still lacking a painting for the wall above the bench seat but, otherwise, it's done."

"You do so much in such a short time — all this and your new songs," Nikos observed.

"Well, I haven't been sleeping full nights because of this surge of energy, and I haven't had you around as a distraction either," she stated as she walked over to him and ran her hands up his chest and linked them behind his neck. "But now that you're here, I think we should make up for lost time."

"Oh, yes?"

"Yes," she nodded and spoke in a seductively soft tone. "I still need to break in my new bed. Would you like to help me with that?"

Nikos nodded, smiling, as he leaned over and kissed her. The softness of his lips and the smell of his skin made Selene dizzy with anticipation.

"I missed this so much," she whispered as she planted another intense kiss on him, wrapping her arms tighter around his neck while pressing her body up against his. Nikos didn't say a word but instead let his hands do the talking as he slowly stroked her back until they reached her hips, where they gripped the bottom of her tank top and pulled it up over her head. As he continued to kiss her, Selene slid her hands down his arms until they found his belt buckle at his waist, which she hastily pulled open before pushing his shirt up over his chest and head. Within seconds of this, she had undone the zippered fly of his jeans and pushed them down to his knees, running her fingertips over his thighs and shaft as she rose again to face him. The teasing lightness of her touch triggered instant arousal that motivated Nikos to take control, so he spun Selene around to face away from him and he leaned over to kiss the back of her neck and shoulders. As he did this, he stealthily unhooked her lace bra, eased the straps off her shoulders and ran his hands around to fondle her breasts. Selene let out a sigh as his touch enveloped her, which only encouraged Nikos to up the ante. He slid his hands down and, in one swift motion, pushed her jean mini-skirt and lace thong down over her hips and rushed her over to the bed as he stepped out of his pants.

Without letting Selene out of his grasp, Nikos lifted her and rested her on her knees in the middle of the mattress and knelt behind her as he continued to caress her chest. Watching him eagerly over her shoulder, she cupped Nikos' cheek with her hand as she kissed him, their tongues dancing with each other in the space between their lips. Her other hand slipped inside the flap of his underwear and began to stroke his manhood. As she did this, Nikos' hands wandered down and began to stroke her pussy and tease her clit, which quickly made her wet and warm, so he maneuvered his knees to push her feet and legs further apart. Right on cue, Selene pulled his penis through the flap and Nikos continued to rub her sweet spot as he slid himself inside her. She let out a moan as Nikos held her body against his and drove himself in deeper but, as his thrusting intensified, she threw her weight forward and gripped the brass footboard for leverage. His strong hands slid down her back and tightened their grasp over her rear. Within minutes, the intensity caused her to involuntarily call out his name as she came for him.

Nikos began to slow his pace and lean forward over her as she tightened, but she was far from done with him. Selene shifted forward and then twisted around, using her body weight to flip Nikos onto his back. With both hands on his chest restraining him, Selene threw her leg over to mount him and began to slide up and down on his cock, slowly at first and then with increasing speed as she felt his shaft swell inside her. Several minutes later, Selene grabbed the bar again and leaned forward until her breasts dangled above Nikos' chin. While he pleasured them with his lips and tongue, he bent his knees slightly and wrapped his arms tightly around her back. As Selene glided back and forth over him, moaning with pleasure, every muscle in her body began to tense up and twitch until the release came, and the powerful climax surging through her caused her to cry out.

"Don't stop, Nikos," she exclaimed between gasps. "Cum with me!"

She leaned in closer and began to kiss his neck and nibble on his earlobe, and the combination of sensations with the quivering of her orgasm sent him over the edge. Nikos let out a breathy groan as he reached pleasure's zenith. Their motion slowed until both of them were lost to the delirium of the moment. Selene rested her tired and tingling body on top of Nikos as he continued to hold her. Their lips met for a few tender kisses before Selene dropped her head to his shoulder. The soft sound of her breathing in his ear made Nikos smile as they passed out on the bed.

* * *

By early evening, they finally woke in Selene's new room. Nikos stirred first and, as he propped himself up on his elbow, he looked down at Selene still peacefully lost in sleep next to him. With the tip of his finger, he brushed one of her curls off her cheek and leaned over to kiss it. He stared at her with soft eyes and a slight smile for a moment more before gently getting out of bed. He tiptoed over to the bathroom, quickly splashed some water on his face and then headed over to the kitchen to start making dinner for them. He quietly searched the cupboards and refrigerator and pulled out two small chicken breasts, a jar of pesto sauce, a red bell pepper, a red onion, a zucchini, a white eggplant, some okra pods and fresh basil. As a bit of olive oil warmed in a large pan on the stove, Nikos quickly cleaned the chicken before adding it to the pan along with the pesto sauce. As it slowly began to cook over the heat, he chopped all of the vegetables into bite-sized pieces and minced the basil and then, once the chicken appeared half-cooked, tossed everything else in with it.

* * *

The smell of food cooking wafted from the kitchen back to the bedroom and woke Selene. She felt delighted to awaken and discover her man in her kitchen cooking for her. She slid out of bed, walked over to her wardrobe to put on the old silk robe and then tied her messy hair back in a loose ponytail before joining Nikos in the kitchen.

"Whatever you're making, it smells delicious," she said after greeting him with a kiss.

"Pesto chicken with vegetables," he said as he lifted the pan's lid to show her.

"First was great sex and now you're making dinner for me in your underwear – I'm a lucky woman!" she said as she planted another kiss on him. "I'll open a bottle of wine for us and set the table outside."

Selene carried some cutlery and plates out to the table and arranged them in place, bringing her guitar back inside to set it on the rocking chair. As Nikos went back into the bedroom to put on his shirt and then returned to the kitchen to stir the pan's contents, Selene pulled a bottle of chilled Nykteri wine from Hatzidakis Winery out of the fridge, removed the cork and poured two generous glasses for them. A few minutes later, once the food had finished cooking, Nikos spooned the dish out of the pan and onto a platter, which he carried outside as Selene followed with the wine. A cool, swift breeze stirred outside pushing thick, puffy clouds over the sea to settle above the island, and the soft evening light reflected off them in a way that gave them a silver hue with creamy yellow edges. The air still felt hot and dry and the combination made for a beautiful summer's evening on Santorini. Above them, the village bustled with people wandering in and out of shops, drinking at traditional taverns and enjoying the sights, but their noise and energy barely reached Selene and Nikos down the cliffside on her veranda, where they settled at the table for a quiet dinner. The meal perfectly complemented the season, with its fresh produce and light flavours blending well with the dry, citrusy taste of the wine, its sustenance reinvigorating the couple as they sat and discussed Selene's new music. She revealed that, of the eight songs now completed, she wrote three of them as instrumental numbers.

"I'm working on a fourth one now," she said, "and it's inspired by you."

"Will you play it for me?" he asked.

"It's only half written right now, but I'm calling it 'Starlit Sea.'"

The song's name said it all and Nikos instantly knew she was referring to the night they had waded out into the caldera completely naked after her birthday dinner. The erotic memories of that first time together and Selene's romantic gesture of immortalizing them in song brought a smile to Nikos' face. She leaned over and planted a spontaneous kiss on his lips. When their lips parted, she said, "Babe, can I ask you a favour?"

"Of course," he replied as they sat back in their chairs.

"I don't have access to a studio here to lay down any samples of these new songs to send along to the label, but I have an idea. I'm meeting Pavlo this coming week to practice some more and I was hoping you could film us performing a few of them. Maybe next weekend? Vicky's office has a digital camcorder I should be able to borrow and then I'll just have to send the video off to Roger. Would you help me with this?"

"I will," he offered.

"Thank you, Nikos," she said as she leaned in and kissed him again. As her fingers passed through his hair and stroked the back of his neck, Nikos slid his hand inside her loosely tied silk robe and gently stroked the curve of her breast.

However, the moment was quickly broken when they became aware of another sensation: raindrops. During the course of their meal, a great host of dark clouds had gathered in the distance and the wind had pushed them steadily toward the island. As they looked out over the caldera, Selene and Nikos could see a sheet of heavy rain falling over the water that would reach them in a matter of minutes to drench the island in a rare summer storm.

"We should go inside," he said and began to collect the dishes from the table. He took the platter and plates inside first and then returned for the empty wine glasses as Selene untied the seat cushions to bring them indoors. While she closed the front windows, Nikos poured more wine and then stood behind Selene as she gazed through the glass at the approaching downpour. Thunder growled in the distance as Nikos handed Selene her drink and slipped his hand around her waist and inside the robe again. He sipped his wine and kissed the back of her neck as she watched the storm make landfall and soak the veranda. As the thunder grew louder and the dark sky was illuminated by flashes of lightning over the sea, Nikos slid his hand down further to stroke Selene's inner thigh and whispered in her ear, "This is one good way to pass a storm."

That one little hint was all the invitation Selene needed, so she turned away from the window and led Nikos back to her bedroom, where they remained for the rest of the night.

Chapter Twelve

By mid-July, a lingering heat wave had hit the island after settling over much of the Mediterranean four days earlier. It scorched Santorini with constant dry heat that was nearly suffocating from an hour after sunrise and made midday almost unbearable. Tourists inundated the air-conditioned indoor venues, trying to spend as much of their time as possible out of the sun, leaving the normally busy pedestrian street running through Oia to suffer a drought of foot traffic. The hot, stuffy shops frequently appeared empty. The restaurants and cafés also struggled because most of their sheltered space did not have air conditioning, relying instead on the breeze coming through windows or open deck space. The pools at the village's hotels were some of the only outdoor spaces teeming with action as the guests made every effort to stay cool.

On Saturday morning, Selene gathered with Nikos and Pavlo at his restaurant, shielded by the covered section of the rooftop patio. She and Pavlo had met there to work on her songs four times in the last week, in the mornings, before he opened Bougainvillea's kitchen to lunchtime patrons. Pavlo had turned out to be a rather inspired choice for a writing partner. Well versed in traditional Greek musical styles but with an understanding of and appreciation for the type of hybrid sound Selene hoped to generate, he could instinctively sense her descriptions of the melodies, rhythms and moods she heard in her head and bring them to life on his bouzouki. He was a gifted self-taught musician and she felt grateful to have his help, and now all of their practice was coming together as they prepared to film the performance of three of her new songs.

They arranged two chairs close together on the small platform while Nikos set his chair a few feet in front of them and straddled it backwards so he could use the top support bar as a balance for the camcorder in the absence of a tripod. Selene instructed him to begin taping each song at a wide-angle view to show her and Pavlo playing together but suggested he use the zoom on the lens to move in as he saw fit during solos and choruses or other such moments.

"I will start by speaking to the camera," she told Nikos, "to introduce each song. Are you ready?"

"Yes," he replied. "Once you want to start, I will signal with my hand that we are filming."

"Okay, let's do this," she said as she settled into her chair next to Pavlo and cradled her guitar in her lap. Selene felt calm, poised and prepared and had grown used to working with cameras after filming many music videos over the years with Kauri Spirit, so her professionalism and experience proved very useful as they readied for the unrehearsed shoot. She felt confident that Pavlo, as a natural performer, could handle such a project and her gut told her that Nikos' artist's eye would make him a good videographer. Selene glanced over at Pavlo, who nodded to her to signal his readiness, and then she turned her head back to Nikos and the camcorder.

"Let's begin."

Selene watched as Nikos turned on the camera, flipped open the LCD screen and focused the lens on her. Once he signalled her with his free hand, she began to speak.

"Gidday and greetings from Santorini," she started. "I'm Selene Doherty and I'm joined here today by my friend and local bouzouki player Pavlo Kafieris. We are making this video to showcase for you my newest endeavour: a collection of new songs that I hope to pitch to you for a solo album of world folk music. This first song is the cornerstone of the collection, with lyrics originally coming from a poem written by my father. It's called 'Sunsets in Oia.'"

Selene counted Pavlo in and they began to play the song. Nikos directed the camera to focus mainly on Selene during the quieter beginning while panning over to Pavlo for short bouzouki solos that had been added between sections of the lyrics. As the verses progressed and grew toward the end, he kept the screen at a wide angle to feature both of them but, as Selene reached the last notes of the song, he zoomed in to close on her face and its sweet, sombre grin. Selene paused for a moment as Nikos zoomed out to show both of them again and then she addressed the camera once more.

"This next song is lighter and boisterous and will feature a great solo midway of a bouzouki battling a mandolin. I will substitute my guitar for the mandolin for this rendition. It's called 'Wanderlust.'"

Selene began by stomping her foot loudly on the wooden platform, followed by a flurry of strumming that went back and forth between her guitar and Pavlo's bouzouki until their notes joined as she started to sing. The lyrics told of a mythical wanderer who sailed from island to island in search of love and a sense of belonging, but who always felt the pull of adventure and the unknown. It was obviously a metaphor for the life Selene had always lived, and Nikos' toes tapped inside his sandals along with the lively tune. Once the song ended, Selene addressed the camera one final time.

"This last tune will be purely instrumental and is unique because I perform it alone. I call it 'Starlit Sea.'"

Her eyes focused directly on Nikos and she offered him a brief but intimate smile that he returned just before she started to play. It began with a rolling progression of soft and sensual chords to represent the steady break of the waves against their entwined bodies. As the pace slowly gained momentum, she added the echoing taps of her hand against the guitar's wooden body near its sound hole woven with increasingly intricate finger work up and down the frets. Nearly two minutes later, the song reached its dramatic and captivating climax as her hands grew closer together, one dancing down the neck in controlled chaos to press the strings while the other's fingertips plucked them at lightning speed until all of the rapid notes blurred together to sound one blasting chord. She paused, allowing it to linger in the air for just a moment, before returning to the same pulsing medley of tones used in the introduction, which she repeated over a few bars and gradually allowed to fade to silence.

By the conclusion, Selene's heart raced from the strain and focus that the song required of her as well as the surge of energy it gave her in return. Nikos remained motionless.

He filmed her lingering silence for a moment more then, when she nodded her head slightly, he stopped the recording and placed the cover over the lens.

"How was it?" she asked as she set her guitar down against the back of her chair.

"Beautiful," was all Nikos mustered.

Selene stepped down from the platform and walked toward him, rested her hand on his cheek and thanked him for his help.

"I'm going to review the footage," she said. "That felt really great so, if everything looks good on here, we won't have to do another take."

She sat down again on the edge of the small stage, flanked by the men on either side of her.

"Pavlo, you were grand to play with. I got such an amazing vibe from having you next to me. Thanks again for this. You're brilliant," she said to him before returning her gaze to the camcorder to play back the fourteen-minute video. The sound quality was better than she expected considering the limitations of the camera's unidirectional microphone, and Nikos' cinematography thoroughly impressed her.

"This looks wonderful, babe," she said to him as the tape ended. "You should have tried your hand at film school."

Selene closed the LCD screen and returned the camera to its case before packing her guitar, while Pavlo and Nikos replaced the chairs at their nearby tables.

"Well, guys, I'm going to head out and meet Vicky at her office to return the camera and forward the video along to Roger and a few of my label contacts. Thank you so much."

"A pleasure, my dear," Pavlo said as he planted a moist kiss on her cheek. "You make me feel like a rock and roll star. Now I go back to the kitchen."

As Pavlo disappeared inside, Selene turned to Nikos and said, "So, do you want to come over for dinner tonight? I'll cook for you."

"I have dinner with my parents," he replied as he stepped over to her and brushed his hands up and down her arms. "I will come down after."

"Good," she said softly as she reached up and

kissed him goodbye. "I'm off then. See you tonight."

With the camera bag in one hand and her guitar case in the other, Selene headed for Vicky's office. Being greeted by the air conditioning felt like a wonderful relief after having to walk in the scorching heat, and she let out a sigh as the door closed behind her. Inside, business appeared quiet and Vicky was one of only two staff members present that day, leaving Selene free to use Vicky's computer to send the video file.

"How did it go?" Vicky asked as she offered Selene her chair.

"Brilliantly – the guys were pros," she replied as she connected the camcorder to the computer. Once the video loaded to the hard drive, Selene compressed it and backed it up on her flash drive before sending it along to Roger and three of her Warner contacts. In the email, she wrote them a brief message:

Hey there ladies and gents,

I'm writing to you to pitch a new solo project I think will pique your curiosity. I'm aware this is a considerable retreat from what I have written with Kauri Spirit but this project is of an especially personal nature. I hope to record and release this music as a tribute to my late parents by blending the styles of music from my mixed heritage. These songs will highlight parts of all of it. I suppose I can best describe it to you as a blend of the folk sensibility and appeal of Mumford & Sons or Xavier Rudd with the energy and versatility of Jesse Cook, while featuring the rhythms and instruments of traditional Mediterranean, Maori and Celtic music. I already have nine songs written and ready to record and it is shaping up to be some of the most pure music I've ever created. For your consideration, I've attached a video that provides a sample of three of these tracks in their most basic, acoustic form. If this is a record you choose to develop, we will fill out the sound with more instruments in studio.

Much love, Selene

In a second email sent only to Roger, she asked him to rebook the outstanding Kauri Spirit tour dates for late August so she could start recording the solo project the following month.

Finished, she and Vicky stepped out to a nearby tavern, Polski Lokal, which had a shaded patio. They sat outside and devoured their lunch of homemade perogies stuffed with mushrooms and cheese, plus fresh salads washed down with beer. Once they finished the meal, Selene paid their bill and walked Vicky back to work before she headed home, planning to spend the rest of the afternoon in the cave-house rehearsing her new songs and working on another original composition. But her plans were interrupted when she reached her veranda and found Andrew waiting there for her.

"What are you doing here?"

"I saw these photos after we talked. Is this the guy you left me for?" he asked as he waved a copy of The Herald at her.

"Let's get something straight, Andrew. You were the one who left me for someone else. And that didn't answer my question."

"After things wrapped in South Africa, I went to Spain to party with some friends and decided to fly down to see you. You wouldn't hear me out on the phone, Selene. You gave me no other choice. I figured I'd take one more shot."

He stood and walked over to her but she swatted his hand away when he tried to rest it on her cheek. "Don't."

"Come on, babe," he begged. "We were so good together. Don't you remember?"

"What stand out most in my mind are those

photos of you with her. If we were so good together, how could you do that to me? How could you let me find out through the press?"

"You think it's easy for me to flip open the paper and see these photos of you?" he yelled as he motioned to the paper on the table.

There's that temper I remember.

"Those photos are none of your business. We're not together anymore, Andrew. And showing up here isn't going to change that." She turned to the side, clearing a path for him to the stairs. "I think you should leave."

"I'm not leaving, Selene. Not until you hear me out."

"I've heard enough, Andrew. It's not going to change anything. The past is the past. Now, you need to leave. I don't want to hear about this again. Just go."

His eyes narrowed and his brow furrowed as he shook his head. The look made Selene nervous. *Don't do something stupid, Andrew. Please just leave.* When he stepped directly toward her, she knew she would not be so lucky.

"I can't leave you. It's not that simple for me," he said as he leaned in.

"Don't!" Selene took a step back and glared at him. "That's not going to happen, Andrew."

"What's wrong, babe? I don't get it."

"That's exactly your problem."

He stared straight at her, his eyes seeming cold and determined, and his voice grumbled. "You were all mine, and you still are." He swiftly grabbed the back of Selene's neck and forced a kiss on her.

Selene pushed him away and slapped him across the face. The force of the sudden blow caused Andrew to stumble back a couple of steps.

"What the fuck was that for?" he cried out as one hand covered his sore cheek.

"That's for thinking with your dick!" she half shouted at him as he sat on the lip of the short, concrete wall outlining the veranda.

Selene started pacing back and forth, resting her hands on her hips as she drew deep breaths to calm herself. After a few seconds, she stopped suddenly in front of him, bowed her head and mumbled, "How did we get here?"

"I don't know," Andrew said softly and shrugged. "That's not how I saw this going. My feelings for you never went away, Selene. All I think about is what I can do to win you back."

"Look, Andrew," she said as she turned to face him, "I understand that you came here with the best of intentions. The things you said on the phone didn't fall on deaf ears. But you must realize I'm not who I was when we were together. You can't even begin to grasp how much my life has changed since we broke up."

"Tell me," he begged. "Help me to understand so we can move past this."

"That's just it, Andrew. I have moved on. I was really messed up after I left you. I couldn't figure out where I went wrong with us to make you do what you did. But since losing my parents, I've discovered I can't waste time on that kind of drama anymore. Life's too short. Something's shifted since I came here and, while it's had nothing to do with you, it's made me realize there's no point in trying to go back. I can't change what's happened; I just have to move forward. And you need to do the same."

"How can I move on if I can't stop thinking about you?"

"You need to focus your energy on something else, whatever will make you happy and improve your life for the long term. I have a feeling you only want me back because you're afraid of being alone. But maybe it would be good for you. It would give you time to think about the choices you made that got you to this place. Then you can learn how to avoid making the same mistakes again. Our problems didn't start with your infidelity, Andrew. I just don't think we were right for each other."

"So, what is right for you?"

"I'm still not certain, but I think I've found a piece of it here, on this island, and I intend to hold on to it. You should go home to figure out what's right for yourself."

Andrew lowered his head and offered a weak nod. *I think I'm actually getting through to him.*

"I'm so sorry I hurt you, Selene," he whimpered. As he raised his head to look at her, she could tell he was holding back tears.

"Andrew, I'm trying very hard to forgive you, but I'm not there yet. I do know the best thing for both of us right now is to go our separate ways. You're not a bad guy, Andrew, but you've made some stupid mistakes and I think you have some growing up to do. But you'll get there. And I hope you eventually find what makes you happy."

Selene watched as Andrew covered his face with his hands for a moment, shaking his head up and down slightly, before he let out a frustrated and defeated groan. He rose slowly to his feet, letting his arms droop at his sides.

"So this is it?" he asked, and Selene nodded her head sympathetically. "Well, I really buggered that up, didn't I? Okay. I should go. I'm sorry for all of this, Selene, but I'm glad you're happy now. Goodbye."

Andrew reached out and lightly stroked the side

of her arm before quickly turning to leave. Selene glanced up to see him slowly climbing the steps to the pedestrian street, his shoulders hunched forward and head hanging low as he walked. Once he was out of sight, she exhaled an exaggerated sigh of relief and stared down at her feet.

I can't believe that just happened.

She turned, grabbed the newspaper from the table and headed inside, tossing it in the trash bin in the kitchen. Even though Andrew was gone for good, Selene felt so wound up and overwhelmed by the confrontation that she could not concentrate on her music. Instead, she sat in her father's chair, rocking back and forth as she tried to soothe her mind.

The afternoon had vanished and the day's heat slowly began to wane to a more comfortable temperature. Leaning forward from her spot in the rocker, Selene glanced at the clock in the stove and realized it was already after six o'clock, so she decided to fix some dinner. Sitting in the hot little house all afternoon and stressing over Andrew's appearance had caused her to work up an appetite. She pulled a small salmon fillet from her refrigerator that needed to be eaten before it spoiled, so she washed it, removed the skin, and brushed it with olive oil on both sides. Placing it on a baking sheet covered in aluminum foil, she sprinkled it with freshly ground pepper and minced cilantro before sticking it in the oven to broil.

As the fish cooked, she sautéed some mushrooms in a bit of butter and lemon juice on the stove and left them to simmer as she chopped a tomato and an avocado. Next, Selene washed a serving of fresh spinach and spread it out over a plate. She topped the bed of spinach with the pieces of tomato, avocado and mushroom and crumbled plenty of feta cheese over them, by which point the salmon looked done. She removed it from the oven and used a fork to pull it apart and spread the flakes on top of the salad. Finally, she prepared a small amount of dressing and drizzled it over the plate, then poured herself a tall glass of white wine and carried the meal out to her veranda to eat.

Selene quickly gobbled the large salad but, as she sat there sipping her wine and staring out at the calm, inviting water of the caldera, she felt a sudden urge to go for a swim. Her mind was still spinning from dealing with Andrew. *Maybe a swim will help me relax.* Figuring that Nikos would not arrive before eight o'clock, she decided to head down the path and take a brief dip at the small strip of beach below her. Selene gulped down the last of her wine, carried her dirty dishes inside then went into her bedroom to quickly change into her bikini. Wearing

Sunsets in Oia

only the swimsuit and flip-flops, she locked the front door and hustled down the steps to the shore, where she kicked off the sandals and dropped her keys on top of them before darting into the cool water. A few feet out, Selene dove into a tiny approaching wave and propelled herself out further as she skimmed just below the surface. When she emerged for air, she was nearly forty metres from the beach so she flipped onto her back and, sculling lightly with her hands to stay afloat, allowed the waves to slowly push her back to land.

Several minutes passed as she floated with her eyes closed, allowing her breathing to relax and match the peaceful, slow movement of the sea. After a while, she finally felt calm so she opened her eyes and swam against the current back to the beach. Once she emerged from the water and collected her sandals and keys, Selene slowly made her way back up the escarpment, humming a tune as she went. By the time she reached her veranda, the sun had sunk low enough in the sky to cause the buildings on the inside of the crescent to cast long shadows over each other. Nikos sat at her table waiting for her return.

"Were you waiting long?" she asked as she crossed the space between them.

"A few minutes," he nodded. "You went down to swim?"

"Yes. I needed to cool down and relax a bit. I had a crazy afternoon. But now I smell of salt." *He doesn't need to know about Andrew. I took care of it and it would only upset him.* As she started to lean over to kiss him, she noticed a package wrapped in silver paper resting on the table in front of him. "What's that?"

"A gift for you, for your new house," he said.

"Nikos, you didn't have to buy me something for the house, not after you spoiled me on my birthday."

"I did not buy it," he revealed. "You said you need art for the wall near the TV, so I made this for you."

"You made me a piece of art?"

"Open it."

Still dripping wet, Selene flashed Nikos a giddy grin and tore away the paper. Inside a simple black metal frame and behind a pane of glass and a thin, white mat rested a new charcoal drawing. At about a foot tall and double that in width, it depicted the Santorini sunset in the far-right section as two figures watched it while standing amongst the buildings above Amoudi Bay. Even though the angle of their bodies left mostly their backs in view, Selene instantly recognized the profiles of their faces – her parents. Nikos had drawn them in the way her father had described in his poem, with their shoulders pressed together as they shared in nature's

Sunsets in Oia

spectacle. She stared at it, wide-eyed, for several more moments as tears began to collect in the corners of her eyes and, when she finally lifted her head to look at Nikos, one escaped from beneath her lashes and streaked down her cheek.

"It's so beautiful," she murmured while trying to choke back the urge to cry. "When did you do this?"

"After you showed me the house, what you changed."

Before he could lean in and kiss her, a cool breeze swept up over the escarpment and made her shiver.

"You are cold. We should go in."

Inside, she set her keys down in a small blue dish on the front corner of the shelving unit and then held the drawing up in front of her at the empty spot on the wall.

"A perfect fit," she said. "I'll have to hang it right away."

Selene set the framed drawing down on top of the shelf, leaning it against the wall, before turning to the back of the house. She pulled a small tool box out from under the kitchen sink, carried it back and set it down on the shelving unit, retrieving a hammer and two nails from inside. Nikos held the first nail in place as she hammered it into the wall, then he held up a level against it as she secured the second one a few inches away. She returned the tools to the box, closed the lid and then lifted Nikos' sketch to rest it on the nails.

Stepping back, she examined it and turned to him. "I love it," she said, throwing her arms around his neck and pulling him in for a long, passionate kiss. "It's perfect. Thank you."

They kissed again for several moments and, as Selene's body pressed against his, she could feel him becoming aroused. Smiling, she pulled away to look in his eyes. "Now, I need a shower."

She returned the tool box to the kitchen and headed for the bathroom. As she reached the door, though, she turned back to face Nikos.

"Care to join me?" she asked alluringly.

He smiled back to her and followed her into the bathroom, where they quickly stripped off each other's clothes and made love as the hot water of the shower rained down on their skin.

* * *

Late that night, as Nikos slept soundly next to her, Selene lie awake and felt the sudden urge to get out of bed. She lightly lifted Nikos' arm from around her and gently rolled over to leave the room. She closed the door nearly all the way behind her and crept into the main room, where she curled up

Sunsets in Oia

in her father's rocking chair. A light breeze snuck in through the open front window and tickled her bare feet as they rested along the edge of the seat. She maintained only a slight motion in the rocker so that its squeaking would not wake Nikos in the bedroom, and as she glanced around the shadowy place her hand began to stroke the chair's smooth arm.

"I don't know how you did it," she whispered to the darkness, "but somehow you found a way to get through to me. I miss you both so much but I know I couldn't have gotten through this without your help. I hope you can hear me and see all that's changed. I just wish you could have been around to share it with me. I love you forever."

Selene stayed in the chair a while longer, half waiting for a response while allowing the wood frame to hug her, but she soon grew chilly and longed for the warmth of Nikos' body again. Standing slowly, she turned and glanced down at the chair until its motion ceased and then she returned to her bedroom to fall asleep in his arms.

Chapter Thirteen

Five days later, Nikos walked down the steps toward Selene's house in a particularly good mood as he anticipated dinner that evening. Today marked his parents' thirtieth wedding anniversary and they had agreed earlier in the month to allow Nikos to plan a special evening out in their honour. He had called his sisters right away, who promised to fly down for the occasion so they could all treat their parents to a fancy meal at 1800, one of the village's most prestigious restaurants. Nikos had reserved a spacious table for the family and, two days ago, when he finally revealed to his parents where they would enjoy their anniversary dinner, his mother got quite excited to have a reason to dress up for a night on the town.

But her next suggestion thrilled Nikos.

"You should call Selene, have her join the family," she offered.

Nikos took this as an encouraging sign.

Now, Nikos was heading over in his best suit to escort Selene to his parents' house for a pre-dinner drink, and he could not help but be happy in his life – the summer had reunited him with his childhood friend and his long-held fantasy had been fulfilled when she quickly became his new girlfriend, and now his family was welcoming her with open arms as one of their own. It all seemed so perfect to him, and it made him grin as he hustled down the steps.

Nikos crossed the veranda to Selene's front door but hesitated to knock on it when he heard Selene crying, her whimper escaping through the open window, so he tried the knob, which she had left unlocked, and pushed the door open.

* * *

Inside the cavehouse, Selene hunched over, seated on the loveseat, and cried into her hands. The sound of the door creaking open startled her. When she looked up to see Nikos standing there she quickly wiped her eyes and sucked back her tears.

"You're early," she mumbled. "I'm not ready yet."

"What is wrong?" he asked as he walked over, crouched down in front of her and held her hands in his.

"Nothing really," she lied. "Some days I'm good but there are others still that end up bad."

"What makes today bad?" he asked in a soft, comforting voice. "Tell me."

Selene looked into his warm brown eyes and his sympathetic gaze encouraged her to reveal more to him.

"This dinner just had me thinking," she started. "Your parents have been together for so long. They've lived through ups and downs. Even with your dad's health, they've kept things together. They're so strong together and they love each other so much. And the way they are with you and your sisters – it just reminds me of my family. I miss having that."

"I know you do, Selene."

"You know, I'm not terribly close with my extended family," she continued after a few deep breaths. "We're all so spread out. It's a hard reality to swallow, realizing Mum and Dad are gone for good. Now I don't really have anyone in my life who loves me the way they did, no matter what."

Sunsets in Oia

Selene hung her head again and tried to choke back the coming of more tears.

"I do."

"What?"

"I love you, Selene."

She looked down at him and her lips slowly parted as a gaping smile of surprise and delight formed on her face.

"I have loved you for years…since we carved our names in the rock at the windmill. I just never told you, but I say it now. I love you, Selene, and you are not alone."

Stunned, her lips fluttered slightly as if searching for words that couldn't escape until they finally curled into a grin again as she leaned forward. Selene wrapped her arms tightly around his neck and kissed him with such intensity that it caused Nikos to fall forward onto his knees. He wrapped his arms around her lower back and they held each other tightly as the amorous kissing continued. After several moments, their lips finally parted. Nikos brushed one of her curls away from her face with his fingers. They stared deeply into each other's eyes for several seconds until Selene exhaled a light laugh.

"I'm keeping your family waiting. I'll change for dinner," she said. "Give me ten minutes."

They rose to their feet and she rushed back to

her bedroom, hurriedly undressed and slipped into the dress she had laid out on the bed. The high boat neck sat just below her collar bone and the garment had an empire waist just under her bust, accented by a black ribbon about an inch in width. The top section sparkled in a royal purple fabric while the skirt of pewter silk flowed over her curves and fell to her shins. After pinning back half of her hair with a metallic, butterfly-shaped barrette, Selene quickly applied a charcoal shadow to her eyelids followed by a light coat of mascara, then highlighted her lips with a dab of berry-tinted gloss. She finished the outfit with a pair of simple silver hoop earrings, the bracelet Nikos had given her and a pair of black, strappy heels.

When she returned to the main room, she asked, "Is this dress okay? It belonged to my mother. I didn't have anything of my own here with me that I thought appropriate."

"You look gorgeous," he said as he wrapped his arms around her waist and lightly kissed her lips. Yet, as he started to lead her to the door, Selene stopped him and rested her hands on his chest as she looked up at him.

"I love you, too, Nikos."

As his lips curled into a smile, Nikos lifted Selene into his arms and kissed her again, their faces held

Sunsets in Oia

tightly together as their lips became entangled in the long embrace. By the time Nikos lowered Selene so that her feet could touch the floor again, neither of them wanted to go out to dinner.

"Come on," she said with a smirk. "Let's not keep your family waiting. We'll get back to this later."

With a broad smile on his face, Nikos nodded, wrapped his arm behind her back and led her out the door.

Pre-dinner drinks at the Kafieris' house were consumed quickly as everyone seemed anxious to enjoy the restaurant. Sophia, dressed in her finest clothes, bubbled with excitement. Georgios displayed his pride, too, as he donned a new dark suit and showed off a rare grin. The women grouped together near the front of the house and admired each other's evening wear as Nikos stood off to the side with his father and watched them with adoration.

"You are a lucky man, my son," Georgios said softly to Nikos in Greek as they sipped their glasses of wine. "You have a beautiful woman there. Don't let her go."

At that moment, Selene glanced over her shoulder at Nikos and mouthed the words, "I love you," to him.

The dinner later that evening at 1800 turned into quite the affair and the six of them indulged in some of the finest food the island had to offer. Set in a restored captain's house constructed in the first half of the nineteenth century, the luxurious establishment had built a reputation for its small-plates gastronomy over the last two decades. With its traditionally decorated dining hall and romantic rooftop garden, it was also one of the most pictur-esque restaurants on the island.

As the sunset faded away to night outside, candlelight warmed their table. Nikos ordered a bottle of wine as soon as they all sat down. Once the sommelier returned from the cellar and poured a serving for each of them, Nikos raised his glass.

"A toast to a very special night. I feel blessed to be here to celebrate my parents and their long history together. I am also happy to have my sisters here so we are all together, and to have my beautiful Selene join us. To love and family."

Selene glanced over and noticed Sophia was nearly in tears as she raised her glass to meet her son's. "Oh, my boy," she sighed. "I'm so glad you are all here."

The rest of them lifted their glasses above the middle of the table and cried out, "Opa!" as they clinked together. Selene blushed and smiled when Nikos wrapped his arm around her shoulder and kept it there until the food arrived.

Sunsets in Oia

A short while later, their conversation and laughter were interrupted when the waiter arrived with the meal. He described each dish as he set down plates of grilled lamb chops with green applesauce, roasted sea bass with sundried tomatoes, fish-roe pie with sour cream, spicy vegetable risotto, pappardelle pasta with cherry tomatoes and capers, peppers stuffed with squid, raisins and rice, as well as fresh greens topped with tomatoes, beetroot and strawberries. The air around their table filled with the aromas of spices, fresh seafood and the sweetness of summer vegetables. It all looked so enticing and a hush fell over the table as everyone's attention turned to satisfying their stomachs. More superb Greek wine complemented the meal and, at Emmelia's suggestion, they also sampled the chocolate mousse, a rich, bittersweet and mouth-watering conclusion to their celebratory feast.

Everyone was in a jolly mood – even Georgios' usual grouchiness had melted away and his happy state improved even further by the sight of his three children picking up the cheque for the expensive dinner. He even gave his wife a kiss on the cheek, a rare public display for him, causing her to blush. Before they left, the owner, Ioannis, approached the table and treated the party to a complimentary round of vinsanto in honour of Georgios and

Sophia's anniversary.

Chapter Fourteen

Just over a week had passed since Selene sent the video proposal. From the night of Georgios and Sophia's anniversary dinner, Selene and Nikos had not spent a moment apart — in fact, they only ever left her bed for meals and the occasional trip down the escarpment to go swimming together in the sea. Their recent declarations of love for each other seemed to have bewitched them in some way and they were inseparable.

As the sun rose higher in the sky delivering its heat to the crescent isle and the couple lay in bed still half asleep, Selene's phone rang. Groggily, she reached over to retrieve it.

"Hello?" she muttered, while Nikos stirred next to her in the bed.

"Gidday, Selene," Roger's voice said cheerfully.

"Oh, good morning, Roger. What's up?"

"I just got out of a meeting here and you're gonna want to hear this."

"What is it?"

By the time she hung up the phone, a grin had spread from ear to ear on her face.

"Why do you look very happy?" Nikos asked.

"That was Roger," she said as she leaned over to face him. "He's just negotiated a contract for me with Warner to release my solo album."

"Really? That is wonderful. And so fast."

"Apparently, the guys at the label loved the new songs so they've decided to let me go ahead with my plan to record it in September after the band finishes those last tour dates," she said as she sat up in bed. "Roger spoke to Ryan and Lewis too and it looks like they're cool with the band taking a break for a bit so I can promote the new project. And our booking agent has already rescheduled five of the seven shows for next month, so I need to return in the next week to rehearse a bit with them before we head out on the road."

Selene's excitement bubbled out of her

uncontrollably now as she leapt out of bed to dress, still rambling on about telling Pavlo the good news and hiring other musicians and booking studios for the recording. "There's so much to do," she exclaimed.

With each word that escaped her lips, Nikos' eyes grew wider and his forehead wrinkled with worry. "Wait," he said as he propped himself up on his elbows. "You are leaving?"

Selene turned around and, seeing the concern on his face, walked back over to the bed and laid down next to him, stroking his bare chest with her hand.

"Nikos, I love you but I still have to go," she whispered to him. "I have to work. I can't keep this house and my flat in Wellington if I don't work. I have to leave but I promise I'll be coming back. We'll just have to do long distance for a while."

"I know you have to go but it is so soon. I wanted you here for the rest of the summer."

"I wish I could, babe, but we still have another week together before I have to fly back, and soon after that school will start again so you'll be busy. We'll make this work, Nikos. Okay?"

He nodded but Selene could see a worried look remained in his eyes.

"And since we still have a week together," she said as she rolled over on top of him, "I think we should make good use of that time."

* * *

The next week flew by as Selene frantically made
arrangements for the band's tour dates in New
Zealand and her upcoming recording session. Pavlo
accepted the offer to record with her and became
even more thrilled when he learned that studio time
had been booked for them in New York.

"You make me a very happy man," he exclaimed
when he heard the news. "I will see Statue of Liberty
and Time Square and go to Yankee baseball game."

Meanwhile, Roger kept busy hiring studio musicians and had already managed to book award-
winning mandolin player Jesse Brock and equally
acclaimed fiddler Liz Carroll. But, for Selene, the
real coup came when Rosendo "Chendy" León, the
Cuban drummer who had been working with Jesse
Cook in recent years, agreed to fly from Toronto to
play as her studio percussionist. Roger had only a
producer yet to recruit.

After New York, Selene told him, she planned
to return to New Zealand to add Maori vocals and
flutes to two of the tracks.

"It's all coming together, love," Roger assured her.
"I hate to admit it, but I think the press coverage
you received because of your parents has somehow
made this all easier to arrange. Everyone wants to be

a part of your comeback."

Selene knew he was probably right. Still, she felt grateful for the support. She did not expect the new album to yield the kind of commercial success she had enjoyed with Kauri Spirit but felt confident that people would see the project was close to her heart and listen to it nonetheless. *Even if it fails, I still have the band to fall back on.*

* * *

On the evening of August 1, Nikos drove Selene to the airport. He barely spoke during the ride. She wanted to do something for him, give him something to look forward to, and as he pulled the car onto the road heading east from Messaria to the coastal airport near Monolithos, the idea came to her.

"You know, the next few months will be busy for both of us and it'll be hard to get together, but I was thinking ahead to Christmas. I'd like to have you come over to my place in Wellington for your holiday break. It'll be nice and warm by then and I thought we could go camping in the mountains, just the two of us, to celebrate Christmas. What do you think?"

Nikos' worried look instantly melted away as he

glanced over at her.

"I would love that!" he said, beaming.

"Good," she replied as she leaned over to kiss his cheek. "See – I knew we could make this work."

When they arrived at the airport, many travellers crammed the compact departures area and little private time remained. Nikos stayed with her as long as he could, helped to check her bags, and followed her to the security checkpoint. As that line inched forward, they stood together, holding hands and staring at each other in silence, neither of them wanting to say goodbye.

Just before Selene reached the point where she must pass through the metal detectors, Nikos ran his hands behind her back, pulled her in close to him and said, "I have to have one more kiss." As their lips met, a rush went through Selene's body and caused tears to form in her eyes. The warmth of his body, the tender embrace of his arms and the sweetness of his lips were everything she wanted in that moment. *I wish I could stop everything right here and not let go.*

When Nikos finally pulled his lips away, his head lingered against hers, their foreheads pressing together. With her eyes still closed, Selene heard Nikos draw a deep breath and exhale slowly, and she realized he was trying to delay their parting too. When she heard him whisper the words, "I love you," she opened her eyes and one of the tears she had tried to restrain escaped. She whispered, "I love you," and kissed him once more, her bottom lip starting to tremble as she pulled away. As if in slow motion, Nikos released her from his arms and stepped back. They exchanged bittersweet smiles and then Selene watched him turn and walk out of the airport.

Once boarded, Selene curled up in her seat and leaned against the wall of the cabin. The humming of the engines taxiing the plane to its takeoff position sounded more like white noise as Selene became absorbed with her thoughts. *Here I go. The wanderlust is taking hold again. And yet this is the first time I've wanted to run off of the plane. Leaving here has never been harder.* She glanced down at the dolphin bracelet on her wrist. As she stroked its surface with her finger, another giant tear slowly rolled down her cheek. *I miss you already.*

As the plane raced down the runway and its wheels started to lift off the tarmac, Selene looked out the window and caught a glimpse of Nikos standing at a secluded spot along the coast near the end of the runway. The engines roared as the plane climbed swiftly into the colourful sky and passed over his head, like a giant silver bird carrying her away on a new adventure. Selene wiped a tear from her cheek as she looked down at him, only a dot by that point against the pale, sandy earth. As the sun dipped into the sea in the distance, she was comforted in that moment by the knowledge that she would see him soon.

Acknowledgements

I feel humbled to have so many people in my life who have been instrumental in achieving the goal of publication.

I must first express my eternal gratitude to my incredible family. I am blessed to have two wonderful and supportive parents who recognized my writing talent early on and have continuously nourished it. I'm also indebted to my amazing sister, Erin, whose endless encouragement means the world to me.

This novel wouldn't have been possible without another very important family member: my aunt, Sharon Lennox. I am so grateful that our writing projects have brought us closer together. If it weren't for your guidance and editing genius, I don't know if any of this would have been possible.

I'd also like to thank the rest of my family and my close circle of friends who have stood by me as I made this dream a reality.

One friend in particular deserves extra credit. Jeffrey Rooney: your editing skills, insightful advice and constancy have proved priceless throughout this process. I'd also like to show my gratitude to Melissa Di Persio for serving as my poetry consultant.

Additional thanks must be extended to Pavlo Simtikidis, my Greek music guru; the Kokkalis family and the entire staff at Laokasti Villas, for making me feel at home; and Rosendo "Chendy" León, Jesse Brock and Liz Carroll, for lending me their names.

I also owe a great deal to the team at FriesenPress for working their publishing magic so I could share this story with the world.

CPSIA information can be obtained at www.ICGtesting.com
Printed in the USA
LVOW13s2341191113

361965LV00001B/19/P

9 781460 229866